T0070135

JUST IN TIME

CONSPIRACY THEORIES:
THE TALES OF THE UNTOLD UNDERGROUND MOVEMENT

ATIKU CHARLES ; ISAAC IDRO

Order this book online at www.trafford.com
or email orders@trafford.com

Most Trafford titles are also available at major online book retailers.

Print information available on the last page.

ISBN: 978-1-6987-1294-9 (sc)
ISBN: 978-1-6987-1296-3 (hc)
ISBN: 978-1-6987-1295-6 (e)

Library of Congress Control Number: 978169871294

Trafford rev. 09/19/2022

 www.trafford.com

North America & international
toll-free: 844-688-6899 (USA & Canada)
fax: 812 355 4082

CONTENTS

AKNOWLEDGEMENTS

This literature is a self-written story authored by Mr. Charles Atiku who took many years to develop the original book and working through a tough environment almost delayed this wonderful project. At some point in time it became very hard and unbelievable that this book would reach out to the readers and Mr. Isaac Idro came in to offer moral support and co-authored the tales of **Just in Time**

I am greatly indebted to Mr. Isaac Idro for the sleepless nights he spent perusing through the original manuscript. His dedication and passion motivated me with new energy to continue writing up the stories and when I was overwhelmed by exhaustion, he took up co-authorship role by producing several chapters that made this book appealing to a wider audience especially in the Western World while striving to maintain the original story as set out by the writer. He solely single-handedly took up the publishing costs from editing to the final book. I do not have a better way of saying Precious Blessings upon you!

The authors would like to thank audience or readers of these heartwarming tales that have thought provoking adventures. Moreover, the actual names used in the narratives capture the subject matter, but they are fictional by nature of the story. Readers discretion is advised, and the sole responsibility of the expressed views remain with the authors ingenuities

DEDICATIONS

This Book is dedicated to my beloved parents Mrs. Keturah Drataru Ezatibo and Mr. Joseph Arimisi Ezatibo both of whom shed loads of light to see me grow into the person I am today. Without their guidance and provisions, I would have joined millions of kids who are wasted along the way of life with no future to hold onto.

Mom has been the spear in my life always reminding me to keep striking as a man as Dad kept his tight grip on my daily schedules to ensure that I do not drift away.

I find it very appropriate to express my love and kindness to my Children, Onan Aita Eldred, Obeti Rayner Atiku, Namirembe Forriet Atiku and Nathan Pleasure Atiku Tumwesigye, may you continue to shine in the Glory of God.

Working in the wee hours of the night with a cup of hot coffee by my table courtesy of Aunt Nester Ayakaka to whom I owe a lot though she did not live to see the fruits of my sleepless nights, her unending love gave me courage during the hard moments when the journey seemed impossible. I have a very large space I my heart for Uncle Gad who is now watching me from another world. Your encouraging words did not come for nothing, I include the name of your only daughter Vivian whom you did not even see eye to eye as a testimony of those precious moments we had together.

Lastly to you my siblings and numerous friends whom I may not mention and thank individually, many thanks for walking this lane by my side.

Chapter I

THE DOCUMENTS AND CONFUSION IN THE ROOM

Nick Morgan was at home in Minnesota, flipping through a pack of dusty papers that had stacked in the safety box in his garage. Still, not finding the necessary file, he stood up and began walking lazily across his bedroom to the living room as if this would bring his memory to the present. Nick had tiny balls of sweat forming along his dirty mane of hair, just above his eyebrows. He wiped them off with the back of his hand. Nick was now startled by memory loss because what Nick thought was that something had slipped through his mind and caused him to fumble in gathering conclusive evidence. He had an old pal whose contact he lost at the moment though needed it most urgently; he knew his fate lay in those dusty and old files. He kept digging from one batch of documents to another, yielding no good hints.

As he was getting weary and tired, he remembered a day in the past where he helped his friend acquire a property from a mortgage firm. Fetching a cup of coffee, he reassured himself that he would not relent on this.

Tossing the empty cup into the sink, he ran several steps from his living room downstairs to the back door. Car keys in hand, he entered the old Chevrolet pickup and drove off to the Country Side to the offices of ROLAND PROPERTIES CONSULTANTS.

After about a one-hour drive, he found his way to an old Patriarch building. At the reception, he was received by a slender and tall lady only called Brenda as specified on the name tag struck against her breast line. He introduced himself and asked to speak to the firm legal officer. After a couple of minutes and explaining why he was here, he was ushered into the office of a short, stout Portuguese American National who identified himself as Emilio Brandon.

Again exchanging a few pleasantries and giving a 100 dollar bill, Brandon agreed to help dig out the file on condition that it was kept confidential. Nick accepted and led to the upper floor in a small tidy room full of filing cabinets and two computers. Another lady worked in this room, and Brandon introduced Nick to her with authority.

Later Brandon spoke to her in a low voice, and the lady excused herself, allowing these two gentlemen time to be alone. Sooner, Brandon logged into the computer system using another account not shared by the staff in his office. Immediately, the names of Linda Bradley came on the screen. She was an old Asian American woman in her late 60s when she was a wife to T.R. Roberts, a well-known and wealthy businessman who dealt in imported electronics. However, his undisclosed businesses were the ivory trade from the Democratic Republic of Congo, Poppy from Afghanistan, Diamond from Namibia, and improved tea from Iran. He had several times appeared on files of the secret agents as an evil man. He had a way of sorting out his dirty past using illicit cash from his various dubious businesses.

T.R. Roberts had several properties in the States, registered under different names; he lived off the coast most of the time. He had a conglomerate of Charity Agencies run under The Caliphs Organisation, which he and associates never discussed with the open world. His preferred countries of residence were the Bahamas, Trinidad and Tobago, and South Africa. He enlisted some young, intelligent guys like Hamish Kumar to run his errands as he lay in the background. Hamish Kumar is a Sudanese American citizen who had worked for Orion Corporation Field. In this renowned illicit sex syndicate, young girls are fetched from Africa and taken to Hong Kong and Malaysia for an underworld business network. They first introduced them to drugs and alcohol before joining the underworld of pole dancing. The nude striper and in bikini entertainers at Brothels and Bars run as pseudo businesses. After getting accustomed to this life, many later upgraded to working as carriers of small units of drugs and dropping scripts to valuable contacts—these nightclubs run by moguls who own several entertainment houses flooded with horrific sexual orgies. The many youths are attacking this sector where they work as transporters and cargo traders on behalf of wealthy gangs. This business started making headlines on media as early as 1984, but many authorities did not believe it because they paid them to ignore it.

After checking in the database, Brandon was able to locate the file number and its particular location. He walked across the room to fetch an old brown file, handed it to Nick, and said, "You are on your own." The two walked down the chamber after logging out of the computer.

Nick drove off and went straight to his house.

On June 24th, 1974, Nick sat in the gardens of a cozy and well-furnished estate of Laria. He seemed sunk into oblivion, for he had no clear vision of what the future held for him. At this particular moment, Nick looked like a Zombie. Getting up, he walked with some pain in the groin as he approached the patio and collapsed into the sofa; he peeped into a space for a long time and could see nothing.

Their criminal activities showed by the sad look on his face and dead eyes.

He had smoked several sticks of cigarettes, and the buts were lying in the ashtray, yet in his hand was a half stick of highly adulterated cigar smoldering off gaily, but he took no chance of pulling at least a puff. He crossed his legs with ease, the leftover the right, his right hand had the cigar, and the left was tucked skillfully under his waist, touching the revolver lightly.

Now his senses seemed to be coming back when he drew at his cigar and blew out the smoke so hurriedly that it took a swirling journey and filled the space around his head, thus irritating his eyes causing him to wink a bit.

Nick undid his legs and started drawing an imaginary map on the carpet. Just at this point, a sharp, piercing voice came from down the corridor on the right side of the rented mansion. It was like the sound of broken glass, which activated his emotions a thousand-fold.

Nick immediately went down on all fours, and the revolver was jutting in his right hand.

He curled by the wall, alert. When he started to move, he saw some smoke oozing from the thick woolen carpet and destroying the delicate fabric of the Turkish product. He stepped on it vigorously. He took a deep breath and held much of the air in his lungs as he paced along with the room; the soles of his heavy-duty shoes made some noise, so he kicked them off. With socks still on his feet, he stealthily sneaked down to his bedroom, where the sound seemed to have emanated. After pacing about ten yards down the corridor, the door was flanked open, and a woman shoved her head thereon. As he raised the gun at her, she screamed.

"Relax !...'

'It's me, Jackie.' Nick stood there perplexed and still held the gun in a firing position.

His eyes glazed wildly towards this woman with a dropped jaw. His mouth kept open as if they had uttered a word. Once Jackie realized that Nick was not in order, she rushed to him and flung her arms around his neck, and kissed him hard to awaken him from his disillusion, but it was a matter of double luck that he never fired at her.

He never bothered to kiss her back, and he was cold when she removed the gun from his hand and inserted it under her skirts onto an elastic band attached to the frontal lace of her panties.

Jackie drew backward and led him to the bedroom closing the door behind them.

Nick sat on the edge of the bed; he held his head and ad with both hands while Jackie rushed to the kitchen, she emerged with a small glass of cold water, and after he had taken a sip, he felt better and sighed with relief as she wiped his forehead with a wet towel. It took several minutes for Nick to regain his full spirits, which worried Jackie greatly.

"Please, I need some coffee... Jackie!" He managed to say at last." These words pierced through the silent and empty room. Jackie excused herself when she returned after a short while, and she found space on the bed by his side. They were sipping from cups of hot coffee; with all the impatience and curiosity of wanting to know the cause of the trouble, she asked, "you are acting strange today. Have you been offered some stone to cook?"

"No... why?" Nick asked.

"You were about to send a bullet through my head when I opened the door to see if you were in!"

"Shit! Sorry, I'm still feeling shaken by the crash of the window, and I forgot that you were in". "I had been in the room since long; the window swung shut with a bang by the blowing wind.

You seem to be thinking so hard today".

She said, rubbing his forehead with her palm.

"My feelings aren't clean, at least! He responded.

The gay evening light penetrated through the silk curtains, and the color that reached their bodies was a little cream. They sat interlaced, snuggling with each other. Jackie began rubbing Nick by the chest, and he never resisted her, though. The calmness of Nick only helped to open the bottle of passion that lay in the depth of his heart. The heat in him had accumulated so tremendously that he let her go and ferry off the tray from which they had been sipping coffee. While she left the Room, Nick got up and stripped off his shirt.

Nick went so close to the door when she touched the knob on her return; he yanked the door open; he took her in his arms and laid her on the bed. He began kissing her and romping with her.

Later he crept out of bed and reached the wardrobe; in the lower partition, he drew a bottle of Red Sweet Wine. He poured a glassful for both of them.

Later, she said, "Nick, you are so good to me." He let go of her. This time, she didn't close her eyes, but she stared at the ceiling.

"Nick, what's your new job or what's wrong with the old one? Jackie asked as a matter of fact.

"No answer! He said tartly.

"I know from the look in your eyes that the whole line may be dirty and delicate, but as a matter of fact, I can lend a hand and keep the whole information between you and me-only; do you see what I mean?" Jackie wearily said.

"Fine, but ask me that question later!" He affirmed.

They were lying naked on the bed, side by side like sardines, and moved none of them to the task of covering them up.

It was June 27th, 1980; the sky was clear and blue all day.

The day was busy such that Nick was nearly losing the sense that he was on a hunting expedition. It had been almost a year since he last came to Johannesburg. After a whole day's walking through lanes and avenues, avoiding police and the intelligence personnel at all times, he retired to relax in one of the affluent pubs to soften his spirit with some brandy. Nick sat at the bar with his back to the counter. He was facing the main door to take a full view of the new entrants and monitor those leaving.

He had drunk several cans of Heineken like fish breathing water and had nearly finished a plate of Egg Curry.

His memory seemed to be striking low, a rare occurrence in his everyday life. The last time in June and just a year after, it was falling on him. He gazed in a dizzy way at the neon light in the room.

He never bothered to see who was near him at that time. When a man dressed in a well-tailored suit approached his table.

"Mind if I shared your table"? The man asked with a way of familiarity. Nick, in his mood of reluctance, accepted him to join his company.

He said, "It's okay by me."

The man, without delay, collapsed heavily into an armchair opposite Nick. The only boundary between them was the table and their different personalities.

"Hello boy, thinking of Dolls Rock Gardens in California?" He inquired.

"Why, who are you?"

"Nick, don't be clumsy. It's me, Griffins, your pal in all ways we have ever lived", the man said.

"Am just pondering about what to do next…." Nick said and started recollecting himself to look clearly at Griff's. He took a long peering into his face, and at last, he sighed relief, proof that this was indeed an old-time friend whom he bumped into under such unbelievable circumstances.

Chapter 2

⌒⋎⌐

THE JOURNEY TO STEPLANDS HOTEL

Griffs is a taxi driver under disguise, but his full-time job is to aid murderers and generally secret organizations. He details suspects' residence, location, security conditions, and extra involvements in their various fields. This information could fetch him a lot of money (Rand or Dollars). He had once joined South African Police but got fired for cases of negligence on duty; he served imprisonment for six years under charges of aiding robbers to escape due to mere breach of professional ethics on his part. However, his torture hardened him up, and when he became a taxi driver, he had seen both good and bad, now he sought extra avenues for money earning and thus aiding secret movements. Nick had stepped on a hot pin, which was almost getting stuck into his feet, but the chance being what it is, he escaped to wave a taxi, and Griffs was the one behind the wheel. He drove Nick away.

"You seem uneasy," Griffs remarked once Nick was in the back seats.

"To Steplands Hotel and faster, please," Nick snapped.

"What's up, boy? He was cut short by Nick's shout.

Listen to what I say!" Nick said breathlessly. They drove on for a few kilometers when Griffs brought the point forward again.

"I am of use to you now, if you can understand and cooperate...." He said these words slowly to cause an impact on Nick. Nick sat upright but said nothing, his hand touching his gun swiftly, but he didn't remove it.

"I was once in a hot pan like you, but when I jumped free at last, I still remember all those who helped me, sorry one of them died, May his soul rest..." Nick interrupted this speech.

"Not with me, I don't go with uncalled for helping hands, no, don't try it on me!

He was angry now.

"That's good, but what you need to know is that the world has its strings that are controlled by those who have money and power, not forgetting influence. If they so wish to squeeze you a little, they first pull one rope, and you are in a freezing hell as is with you now". He slowed the car a bit; he then negotiated the corner and headed for the Hotel, some twelve kilometers away with an expansive golf course and an amusement park.

"Hurry up, you lunatic!' Nick said again."

"That's my right title, for I was once in the Police but..." Nick moved uneasily on hearing the word Police. The revolver was already in his palm, pointing at the neck of Griffs.

"Relax, that's not the best idea, nor is that Hotel a better place for you now, but I would suggest let me take you to my private house, and you will be fifty times safer than you could be in that messy Hotel!

The suggestion for going to a private home softened Nick a little, and Griffs continued with his story. During my time in the Police, there was a day six thugs ran out of custody, and my commander pointed an accusing finger at me. Little did I know and say that it was a camouflage, which landed me in the cells for six years.

That's where my spirit hardened beyond ordinary misery.

Also, it is the reason why I am on my own, living in a separate world of commoners, where you sit together in bars and drink like a fish in a lake.

At this time, they were level with the Steplands Hotel.

"Do I drop you here or..." Griffs asked.

"Just briefly, I want to grasp my few belongings, and off we go with you, "Nick said in a song like Jargon.

He disembarked from that taxi, went into the Hotel, whisked off all his bags and briefcase, and made an exit through the Patio.

The night was cold; there was no one out there at that hour of the night. He had jumped over the fence and waved to Griffs, who was waiting a few meters away from the Hotel's frontal view in his car.

He entered the front seat, and his bags lay in the back seat.

They drove in silence to Griff's home far away, isolated in the high mountains, a forested area where human beings are sighted only from afar. When they were five kilometers to the four four-bedroomed apartments, Griffs stopped the car, removed the taxi sign from the top of the cabin, and placed it on top of Nick's bags. They drove on till they were safe behind locked doors in the house, sipping strong coffee. At this point was the time he resumed his narrations.

"All that I've told you and you have seen for yourself is that I live here alone, and no one knows that I'm here except for the two of us who are here now. I live a life that is so detached from social events but always near high-profile agents.

Griffs talked at length about how he lost his job, his beloved ones, and lost the trail of his girlfriend, one called Monica Hope Beats.

The long talk by Griffs softened Nick further, and he talked with ease and revealed the ordeal of the night and Griffs promised they would draw a plan in the morning and he would help Nick out of the country.

In the morning, Griffs opened an old Television, and from the box, he removed a dirty and yellow piece of paper that contained a list of assassins engaged by The Black Hawk. He informed Nick that these groups are wholly dealing in arms from China and Russia. Their main port of trafficking included Maputo and Port Elizabeth. Most of their bad boys lived in Mozambique and only came into South Africa for business. Their head of covert operations is one called Peter, who doubles as a dealer of stolen cars.

The South African Police have secret deals with these boys, so it was dangerous to step on their toes. He gave Nick all this information, as he earned $1500 for accomplishing the mission, and warned Nick never to step back into South Africa without checking out what's across this part of the land torn apart between the whites and the blacks and restricted by the river of apartheid. The secret revelation all went into Nick's head, and he promised never to mess around anymore.

That was how they had met and departed.

Some two years down the road, the secret agent called Nick on a particular assignment to the South, and this time around, Griffs wanted his hand in a dirty job.

"Oh, Griffs, have you been going bonking as usual?" Nick asked.

"No, I am a transformed person; these days, I'm out of that line of action; I don't even remember when I last kissed a girl," Griffs replied. "Do you mind a glass of wine or a bottle?"

Nick suspends the idea, "I am here on business."

Griff's face-hardened with fear and shock, "Let's move into the lobby and have some talk."

"Even here is okay," Nick said recklessly.

Griffs said this with anger while touching Nick's hand: "We need to get out of here, or we go into the lavatory."

After a couple of minutes, Griffs started at last after seeing no success in persuading this hardcore rascal whom he couldn't do without, in his soon-to-be Manhunt job, "Okay, listen very carefully." He continued, "There's a bird, often sneaking to tap on the gains of Mr. Jones, downtown this bird is a true thunderbird.

Sorry I am not using the right words for reasons I know and predict you understand.

Moreover, the ton of information is worth $150 million US Dollars, contracted in Jones name. Griffs turned to see if there was a man within a hearing distance or anyone attentive like a wily sniper, finding no cause for alarm; he resumed his narration". This bird is sending his agents, thieves to scrap this honey cont.... intent for Jones. So our fear is if the circuit discovers, Mr. Jones is in a firepot - Hope you are getting me!" The story ended sharply, and he caught Nicks' eyes fixed on a man seated in the opposite direction, turning his back towards them. He didn't even ask nor confirm his doubt but openly realized a fit of threatening anger grow in Nick. At last, he saw Nicks' lips move in a murmur of some words of which he was not exactly sure.

In Nicks' head was a confused image of some Afro Arabian goons seated on the far end table taking some soft drinks of some kind? Among them was Hamish, T.R Roberts's most trusted agent; he runs a network so dangerous that the Police feared him personally. He connects well with the white community and the black community. Nick now concentrated by narrowing his eyes, knowing, "this man with a weird beard tossing glasses of water with his tablemates is going to die tonight; he decides to say a conditional "goodbye" under the barrel of the revolver.

He must be eliminated at all costs and in any way because he forged a Delivery certificate worth millions in the names of Mr. Jones".

Nick's line of thought hardened, and he asked. "How many days do you give me for the job?"

"Perhaps not more than three days. Remember, we need positive results only." Griffs replied.

"What are the other terms of the deal?"

"Details will remain between our jaws, but not here. Let's get out into your car," Griffs suggested. "I was driven here by a friend who has left many hours ago." He had lied because he had no friend apart from Nick, nor did the stranger use a taxi, because Police were on the lookout so, he walked into this bar.

"Okay, choose between the lobby and lavatory"! Griffs at last declared. "Lavatory," Nick said. Nick and Griffs walked out of the bar. Then disappeared into the bar corridor on the left of the counter. The Barman took a long inquiring look at Nick, but his action got terminated by the arrival of a couple leaning against the counter and ordering some drinks known to be out of stock. The tactful disengagements were a deliberate attempt by Griffs to distract the attention of the Barman from whatever was happening in the Hotel. The new couple was Griff's close associates Emmy and his call girl, one Joanna.

Johanna was a long-time prostitute in Durban before she joined this clandestine business. She was recruited by himself and taken to a Rehabilitation Centre. She got employed to run one of the numerous child care and orphanages operated by T.R. Roberts as his business face in Mozambique in Chikwalakwala. She lived in a moderate house with sound finances. It would portray a perfect image to the community and Government that she was a genuine humanitarian. She often dined and wined with the politicians and enjoyed good favor from the Religious circles in good volumes. She offered a splendid service to hundreds of orphans and vulnerable children.

She often would slip out of the country to do errands in South Africa, Angola and travel to the United States for professional coaching. Most of her training operates by private hands that are in Boston and Dallas. She is so good at picking intelligence information, and her skills in handling guns would leave several trained Police in terrible doubt.

Emmy was a former hitman in Mozambique and got into trouble when he mismanaged a planned execution of a top politician down in Cape Town; he was arrested and jailed. Moreover, to understand the complexities of cross-boundary connections of criminal syndicates between Mozambique and South Africa, high-profile in-mate prisoners in Cape Town are wealthy convicts. They hired prison consultants to help them gather information on human rights for defending themselves in the process of rebuttal charges against them. Making sentencing lighter, securing releases, reviewing casework, petitioning for perks, and taking midnight calls from frazzled families in a game known in prison circles as handholding. It involved trading in legal matters for up to $100,000. The successful bail relieved families and convicts of the stress associated with imprisonment and losing control over themselves and businesses. Many Ex-convicts established fake organizations claiming to help restore self-esteem and dignity by giving prisoners Bibles and Qurans; this was a ploy that enabled them to move in and out of prisons after securing confessions from inmates, and this information is a sell-out to the families. A well-facilitated legal team assembles, beating the humble work of the jurors. They worked in close networks with Churches and Mosques arranged most of their meetings they often passed as honest and harmless citizens but behind their back is a horrible plan of criminology ranging from extortion, kidnappings, murder, and espionage. Griffs met many bad boys through this system. He learned that many young boys commit petty crimes to get arrested and imprisoned. They linked up with hardcore criminals- "Masters," a brainwashing and training scheme that they loosely call Industrial Bearing takes place while in jail. The training gives them access to contacts and fundamental knowledge of how to execute missions for cash. When completed, they come out with very sophisticated ideas and plans that baffle the most trained police officers and a jury team. They have created a passion for knowledge; no matter how hard-pressed they are, all will get what they want through the long-term process.

The level of unemployment among the blacks was so rampant that they justified their attitude through a highly scandalous lifestyle. Moreover, the experience of unemployment and center for dropping off application forms is where Griffs met him. With the flourishing cash from T.R. Roberts, they bought their freedom through an aging and influential police officer. They transferred from a state detention center in Cape Town. The officer procured relocation to Johannesburg, where some well-positioned bunch of hired secret agents whisked them off. This escape left four police officers dead. So many news runs on the state media, but no arrests came to fruition since they escaped through Musina Bridge to Zimbabwe. They were accorded hospitality in a farm secretly owned by Williams and some Top Politician. They lived on the farm for three years, enjoying complete freedom as they established more contacts for the numerous assignments awaiting them. They traveled to Harare mostly at night to refresh themselves and meet more critical communications.

The couple ordered some blended fruit juice deliberately, knowing it wouldn't be available. "Sorry it's out of stock, but we can serve you lemon juice." She accepted the offer and paid for a glass. Her colleague made as if to turn off but seemed to have remembered something. He ordered some gin, dry, please!

"That stock is not available, Sir," said the Barman,

"Then some white wine, please," He said. He was more cautious of delaying the Barman further as such would make him nervous, but the schedule was well in hand, so Nick and Griffs disappeared into the dark corridors of the Hotel, and their mission was according to plan.

Unnoticed to them was a man dressed in dirty jeans and a black leather jacket on top of a black T-shirt.

The poorly dressed man was Clarkson Noels, a hired agent whose job was to bump people he preferred calling idiots. He is a retired Ranger who had worked over thirty years helping top politicians smuggle ivory out of South Africa to the Asian Countries and China; in return, they would receive vast supplies of weapons, which got the ready market in Angola and Mozambique. He had done several deals for The Caliphs Organisation as an undercover agent while still active in the Rangers. He had lots of foreign contacts, which he accumulated during his service as an active Ranger. He spoke almost all the local languages in the South, like Zulu, Shona, Xhosa, Ndebele, and Afrikaans. He was well versed in all aspects of political, social, and economic life in the South. He divorced Diana Penelope, and his kids lived in the United Kingdom. They went to posh schools. Clarkson was at the center of the bar hall, talking to the Barman, but his gaze went through the faces in the bar in a rapid shot, and he seemed unsatisfied for not getting the one he had come to see. He turned abruptly to the Barman, but the latter was too busy attending to some more customers. Clarkson Noels was to wait for yet another couple of minutes. In the course of waiting, he glanced at the display behind the bar; it matched with all brands of different types of drinks, both strong and light. At the extreme right end of the counter, fitted onto the wall, a large clock indicated 11.00 pm. When Clarkson turned to the Barman, he found the Barman taking along look at him. The Barman almost scared out the last hope of confidence in him.

"Excuse me, Sir; I am looking for a friend who calls here very often." He spoke fluent English. Before he could continue, he was interrupted by the bar attendant.

"I don't think if I can help you in that line, we have no one calling for reservations in the rooms for the whole day, except for these you can see (soothing their throats with drinks)." He stopped suddenly and waved his hand in the direction of those seated in the bar.

But before he could eliminate this man's request, his hand reached into the drawer, and he placed a large blue file on the counter and was fumbling through the papers knowing whom he was secretly searching.

Then Clarkson said, "He's Bremen Collins - aka Griffs!" The Barman was already looking at him quizzically. They all concentrated on peeping through the list of bookings, but their efforts were of no avail. Clarkson retired and proposed a drink for himself. He went and sat at the far corner, where a dim neon light was shining.

The tables in that corner were vacant.

He sat there and waited for a drink. After asserting himself to the chair's comfort, a plump lady dressed in a service gown approached his table, pushing a tray of Bacara.

He raised his eyebrows in appreciation, but the lady only replied to the professional characteristic with a light smile. She disappeared to serve others far beyond the center of the room, but this man could not see elsewhere. This lady had large plume-shaped breasts, heavy buttocks, and as for her hair, they were long, dark, attached into one flop with a pin, the color of the pin matching her underdress. She had a long pointed nose, a torso well-shaped.

"Good for kissing!" Clarkson whispered to himself, lighting a cigar. Before he could continue to outline further the morphology of the lady, Griffs appeared from the corridor, Nick followed him.

Both men who dressed in well-cut suits, black and brown, respectively stood in the background.

Hamish had called in Bright, a chief assassin of The Caliphs Organisation under T.R Roberts. His major jobs were eliminating key opposition politicians, members of Trade Unions, special public interest representatives, and any other person who seems to be a danger to them or makes the mistake of crossing their operation paths.

The Caliphs organization enrolled Mr. Bright because of his diverse knowledge and experience as an ex-ranger and once linked to a terrorist cell in France. He later crossed to the Americas, but he could not escape the telescopic eyes of the CIA and FBI.

After getting asylum in Mozambique, he came down South and settled as a local person and registered as a former British journalist who had retired from active duty and wanted to retire as a freeman. Moreover, the choice was the type of man Hamish wanted for T.R. Roberts. He now knew this particular man Clarkson Noels, but his original name was Michael Pierre Musaikwa.

As a hired gunman, he was always as sharp as a cat, and he had no remorse as he cared less about the lives of those he has so far deprived unjustly.

Griffs had reached the table and seated himself on the chair. He put his right hand in the coat and was happy his 48 Special was intact. He sighed happily and picked a stick from his packet of camels. He got a gas lighter from the pockets of his trousers; after lighting the stick of cigarette, he began pulling vigorously.

Nick joined him at the table, and the same beautiful girl who served them followed him. "Some coke," Nick said. Coke was his favorite beverage that he usually can't abandon on the table for a minute.

They began discussing social issues. Joanna is the girl seated just on your right hand, three tables away; she was once my girlfriend, but later she proved a slippery character.

So I had to chuck her, but since she had known much about me then, I made a deliberate incidence where she bumped into Emmy, the boy seated with him at the table. Emmy was with me in Police, but his problems were minor; he deserted on his own. Now he works for me as an extra pair of eyes-then counts that of Joanna as well!

"That's why they are here. To see what my eyes have missed!" He stopped suddenly to see through the faces in the bar.

"Hey, let me ask if you are married"! Griffs continued realizing that Nick was listening attentively.

"No girlfriend or..." Griffs asked.

"None, but just a few that I bumped into, and it was the end of the story," Nick replied. "You are a smart guy," Griffs replied while taking a sip from a cup of coffee.

"Maybe," Nick said. They chatted for several more minutes, punctuated by instances of laughter and light smiles.

At 12:25 pm, Mr. Griffs stood up and announced his departure and proposed meeting Nick the following day at The Community School Recreational Ground. He walked smartly out of the bar after shaking hands with Nick across the table.

As he was a meter away from the exit, he touched his right shoulder, a signal to his friend Emmy and Joanna that all was right at the moment. He disappeared into the darkness, and minutes later, a heavy motor engine faded with distance. He didn't notice that the most dangerous man around was in the house.

Inside the bar, Clarkson walked to the counter and paid his bill. He went past the counter to the lavatory and seemed to take too long there. Clarkson had sent his small handbag through an accomplice, and now Clarkson was busy checking his weaponry and sets of ammunition. Satisfied with his preparation, Clarkson tacked the pistol under his waist pouch and the extra magazines he stuffed into the pocket of his denim. Clarkson picked his hand gloves, a pair of night vision glasses and gently walked back to the bar. He noticed that the people he came to keep an eye on had left their table except for one man reaching his table. Nick was heading towards the staircase, a clear indication that he had booked here.

Then Emmy and Joanna walked out of the room. The couple stood on the pavement for a minute till they were able to wave a taxi.

Nick grew tired and drunk. He had spent most of the day traveling, meeting agents. Now he needed to go into bed and sleep.

He stood up and paid the Barman. He went straight into the flight of stairs on the left of the corridor. He paced two stairs per stride. Reaching the second landing, he almost bumped into the emotional distance of a drunken couple that was caressing each other, kissing and whispering. He thought of intervening in this nonsense when he was only halfway, but his sacred senses altered his thinking. He went on and dismissed what had occurred in his mind as simply a mood of "stupid jealousy!"

He passed through the narrow space between the walls of the entangled couple.

As he raced to face yet another set of steps, the guy who was kissing with his girlfriend turned abruptly and followed him with a small Wesson and Smith ready at hand. He walked further up the stairs, which brought him to a door labeled "Business room" just behind Nick. He raised the gun to aim as Nick turned with the keys in his hand, on hearing a small click; he jumped towards the wall like a hungry lion and sent this man down with two shots taken at very close range. He cut him on the right shoulder, missing his head narrowly. As Nick prepared to send another bullet, Clarkson was right there in the corridor with a pistol in hand aimed at Nick. Nick rolled on all fours as he sprayed a volley towards Clarkson, now bent on his knees. Nick missed him but remained in a shooting position as they all scampered to get a better view in the dimly lit corridor. Nick took this as a chance to run up the steps, which brought him to the landing of the third floor. He was now standing next to a power control circuit box and next to it were lines of fire extinguishers. He opened the power panel and plugged out two fuses randomly, which sent the floors down into abrupt darkness; he picked a 5 kg fire extinguisher and removed its pin; Clarkson just emerged at this point, walking steadily with his back to the wall. Nick fired a spray of carbon dioxide onto his face sending him chocking to the floor. Then Nick pinned him with a bullet that went right through his left arm. As Clarkson went down in pain, he tried his all to regain control, Nick had already added more gas on him, and Nick disappeared further upstairs.

He ran so fast that he was next to a window that lay open in front of him. Then he remembered his luggage was in the room, so the best next thing was to retrieve them and run away. Another instinct told him, this room might possess ears that he never wanted to come into contact with during rescinding time.

He ran over one more collection of steps and turned right where a long corridor lit with a blue bulb restricted his vision. He moved down the aisle and kept checking the room numbers written on small copper plates. He drew his keys and was able to see the tiny letters printed on the key holder, 325 BR.

On the left side of the corridor, he found his door at last.

He inserted the key, turned it, and the lock clicked open.

He turned the knob, pushed in the door in fury as he entered, and switched off the light. Everything appeared usual. He closed the door firmly behind and locked it immediately.

He did not need to delay any longer in the room if the security systems at the Hotel were alert. He could hear some footsteps of someone running outside in the corridor.

After moments of hurried action, he changed into a new set of clothing, packed all his belongings neatly, tidied the room a bit and picked his lock from the door, and shoved it into his pocket. He unleashed the window and swung it open. All he could see was a dark wall running several stairs up to the room of a high building.

In the dim moonlight, Nick could catch sight of the sewage pipe that formed a network on the wall below and above. He retreated into the room, opened his case, and got his rubber gloves and neckties.

The gloves he put on and went to clean up his fingerprints on the wall. He came back and used the ties for tying his luggage onto his waist.

He came out of the window and started the vigilant move downwards using the sewerage pipe.

Nick lowered his body until his legs rested on the pipe running horizontally. He began moving across the wall till his right hand touched another line from behind the window. Balancing his weight carefully, Nick let go of his grip on the window frame. He began with his hands on the pipe, moving sideways slowly, one leg after the other, moving his hands accordingly, supporting all limbs above and below. Nick reached a junction of the pipeline, here, the double line of pipes he had been using stopped - instead, a larger pipe ran vertically downwards. Without an alternative, even parachuting was yet risky from all that height.

Nick heaved himself onto the trunk of this pipe.

After straddling it, he started a gentle sliding downwards. He made it so slowly that he checked excess momentum initially; this brought him one and a half stairs down. Now a sideways branch confronted him. When he was testing the firmness to relax a bit before another hefty sliding, his feet kicked onto the window frame below the pipe. The commotion aroused the attention of those inside the room.

He could hear them.

Lad, there's someone at the window," said a woman's voice.

Nick nearly froze in shock as he heard the whispers. After a pause, someone was turning in bed, and a man's voice uttered some confusing sentences which Nick could not get well.

Then in a sheepish voice, he heard the man say," Darling, you might have dreamt." And soon after a moment, those inside were rumbling in the bed – "Sex!"- Nick predicted, as the girl screamed a profound cry of ecstasy.

"Idiots!" Nick rebuked himself. He tried to assume that these were the couples he had got in the corridor that night some hours ago. He waited for them to fall asleep. Nick turned to see below and saw the flower gardens down the cliff showing clearly under the moonlight.

He estimated his position - only some ten feet. He thought fast and let go of his grip on the pipe - in a summersault, he tumbled and landed foot quickly in the garden. The weight of the luggage swung him forwards, and he fell with his face down.

He was not hurt. He got to his feet again and ran as fast as his legs could allow to the nearest avenue escaping the scene of horror.

At this time, as Nick glanced at his watch, he got the shock of his life to find it was 3.47 am. He raced his brain very fast and undid the luggage from his waist. Nick held the bag in the right hand, the briefcase in the left hand, and his shotgun well tucked in his breast pocket of the coat. He steadied his steps a bit and stopped to wave a taxi.

It was unknown to Nick that it was Emmy in the car, the same car as Griffs, but why this coincidence as he was fumbling for words to give to the driver, which address and the like.

As he seated himself in the car and laid his luggage on the backseat, he said, "To Jeff Highlands." The driver turned to see in his direction and engaged the forward gear.

They drove in silence for several kilometers. The long drive brought them out of the town, and they were in the calm outskirts of the city where the traffic was less and lights decreased considerably.

"Trouble again"? Emmy asked.

This question jerked Nick wide awake to full alert; his mind was racing in overdrive as he pondered his way out.

"Not quite; I changed my mind." That was all Nick managed to say.

"You are not taking the job you mean."

"Which job, who are you? I don't know what you are talking about".

"I am Emmy, Griffs' friend. Do you know that you are in Griffs' car? The questions asked were deliberately said slowly to allow him to capture the words.

"Okay, cool down; I was present in the hotel last evening with a girl."

I saw you with Griffs, and I know what you talked about"!

He stopped suddenly to give time to Nick to check his memory well.

"You mean you came here to keep an eye on me all night?"

Nick asked, anger rising in his voice. He felt clumsy having asked this question. How could Griffs pin every action to Emmy? He kept wondering how this kind of trade is running here.

"That's it!" Emmy said. "Learn to ask me fewer questions."

Nick settled down and left things to happen as they planned.

At last, he said! "It was good of you to be around."

"That's part of my job, and it earns me a meal," Emmy said.

"You and Griffs seem to make the two of you, and that's why you are one, I suppose?" Nick said

"You are right" watching at the dashboard clock, Emmy continues, "Let's get done there in a few minutes for safety." He pressed the accelerator further and the old Chevrolet well on the road.

As they were moving uphill to the isolated house, Emmy switched off the headlights, and he flashed it fully, again off and on and lastly off, then he drove on with the parking lights only. Immediately he stopped the car as they were in the well-maintained smooth gravel with a few flowers lined along the walkway, the front door open. Somebody was standing there, but since the lights in the house were off, Nick could not tell who that person could be. Before he could think of picking his luggage, Emmy had already reached for them, and the engine had stopped running. Nick was able to see a tall giant male figure in the darkness. The tall man was Griff's guard at home, and he was always handy if there was work at hand. At this time, Nick knew he was mistaken to think that Griffs had opened the door and was the one welcoming them. As they entered the large spacious living room, Griff's voice came authoritatively in the chilling night,

"Done, boy, both of you get seats."

"Some coffee, please, Joan?" He commanded, and the girl sort of swirled herself round and disappeared into the oval kitchen. Nick and Emmy sat down; meanwhile, Joanna arrived with some glasses and a hot flask and served the three men. She attempted to carry Nick's luggage.

"Don't touch! Good girl" The two men turned to look at Nick as he waved to Joana. She obeyed his orders without question and left the three men to their own.

"I told you to be more careful yourself," Griffs chipped in

"I've tried my best to."

"But why all this mess."

"It was rather my question. I had a right in the corridors. Nick tried it on me, and I pinned him somehow there. So what was all the mess about?" He took more time to explain mainly what occurred and what he did.

"I knew you would have problems, so I sent Emmy to keep a watch."

"I'm pleased to hear that," Nick said.

They all sat quietly to sip the coffee.

As they finished conversing, Griffs was the first to speak out and asked: "Emmy, go back there on your Motorcycle and clean the hotel record book - no mess about that. See you in the morning. I just want some time with my guest", after smoking cigarettes, Emmy left the house and headed away, all along saying no word. The enigma reckoned in Nicks' mind why Emmy had warned him to learn to ask fewer questions.

Nick and Griffs sat in silence in about twenty minutes sipping coffee, and when they talked, Griffs first broke the silence.

"I gather, you do go with little sleep?" Griffs asked.

"It's okay, even if I don't go to bed till morning."

"That's fine, to begin with; do you know how I knew about your arrival in Johannesburg and which hotel you could probably call in?"

Griffs asked, keeping his voice low and steady.

"I can't tell, but it seems you have high links. Let me also ask you. Last time you told me you are well apart from the world, especially its people, how come to Emmy and Joanna...?" He was cut short.

"It is not a good idea to stay all alone, and it is likewise not bad to keep contact with a few who can tip you on events happening here or elsewhere."

"That far we are together," Nick said after a long pause and consideration.

"Fine, I have many contacts, but my private residence is not known to them.

For your information, Emmy and Joanna have come to know of this place only last evening.

I must assure you that. I have weighed the consequence two hundred times over; that's why they are here. The time was 5:45 am. Griff took Nick to the spare room, and he retired to his own for the remaining hours of the morning.

"Nick, breakfast is at 8.00 am". He went to his room.

Chapter 3

~~~

AT THE ROULER BRENT
HOTEL IN PRETORIA

Nick had first finished checking his rounds - it was packed. He took a glance hurriedly at his watch. And the time was 9:20 p.m. only- some ten minutes to the beginning of the meeting. T.R Roberts runs the sessions of The Caliphs Organisation.

The number one dirty organization in the Southern States, it was well-coordinated, and most of its members stayed abroad. They only came down to the south if there were matters on the ground that required them in cases of urgency. Moreover, such business ventures required professionalism; most of their businesses were carried out by some hired and trusted hands under the supervision of Griffs, who rose in the ranks to be the only known highest member living on the ground. The preparations had gone on for a long time till the last date drew nearer. Griffs had been monitoring all their arrangements. He worked so hard to keep his colleagues well informed of the progress. He had briefed Nick thoroughly well about the plans he had formulated with his group to eliminate this group of bastards.

The Caliphs had a meeting at Rouler Brent Hotel at Pretoria. Moreover, it wasn't an up-market place, but the choice was unique and well-intended purpose than usual luxury. It had a sizeable serene compound, a forest of artificial trees and flowers. This large old-fashioned storied building housed the restaurant, bar, indoor sports arena, and a gym, all seated on the ground floor. Then the self-contained rooms were upstairs, and upon the rooftop was a helipad reserved for specific clients. The hotel belonged to a Boer who now runs a chain of amenities businesses across Southern Africa and the Caribbean.

He enjoys affluent clientele because of his earlier political life, and now retired, he spends most of his time playing golf and listening to Afro Caribbean music. He is married to a young Afro Canadian lady called Esther, who is genuinely a patriarch descendant, and she worships this rich background with absolute discipline. She was extremely loving and caring, many friends found her affection too warm and inviting, and they revered her for this open attitude. They bore no kids but have a benevolent heart that they extended to many children and families without reservations—always comforting and gladly giving fortitude to those who needed their hand.

It was dark, and the cold breeze outside was intolerable as Nick stood panting in that well-maintained compound of the hotel. At this exact venue, the meeting was going to occur, he murmured to himself several times, affirming courage for the job at hand. Mr. Griffs always enjoyed handling such dangerous duties single-handed because Griffs feared some dubious partners who could let you in trouble in no minute. The sneaky acts only reinforced his convictions so much that he never saw the lights of a drawing blue Datsun approach the entrance to the hotel. Just as he bent low to hide amongst the flowers, a second, yet a third car drove in, and he seemed satisfied that his prey was a handful for the night and he only needed to calm his nerves and focus his mind. He remembered the few words of his one-time associate now dead, "Let the birds settle so that you can take a good aim.

Don't scare them away by mistrusted shots" Walter uttered these words after three bullets had sunk in his chest and there was blood in his mouth, his head rolling upside down. He had died that way after talking. They had gone with Nick on a fateful night to ditch on Joyce Fender, a seasoned and highly daredevil spy who had walked

The Americas, Europe, and Africa with equally daring missions open the identities of Walter, Nick, and Griffs. Her special mission was to find out who were those guys that worked with him. That time it was Walter who aimed, and it was so captivating and so good, but the only problem was that Fender reacted fast before she died; she sprayed volleys of bullets on the attackers - Walter was dead.

Nick continued remembering all these agonies that had befallen them. The confusion gave time for the ten men in the house to take their seats. These men were seated in the board room of the Blue Hotel Lovelier. All of them dressed in an orderly way as if to reflect their hierarchy in the organization.

Four men dressed in black trousers and black leather jackets were at the scene of the carnage. Two men in black suits with black shirts and a white necktie were members of the team.

One was wearing a gray suit, and the other was in a white suit with a red necktie.

The one in white was at the head of the table; the one in gray was on his left, where a row of four other men sat. On the right of the table were four men, all in black trousers and leather jackets.

Most of them wore dark glasses except the boss. He had small round narrowed eyes that often cut piercing glances at those in the room.

Nick moved stealthily to the hindquarters of the hotel but came back after finding too much light there. He had anticipated crossing through the hotel patio and verandah, but this was equally unpleasant and risky. He had assembled a homemade explosive fitted with a microchip under the supervision of Griffs, and they managed to connect on to a small Microphone. The timing was that should there be any sound of specific decibels, it would blow up. It was the duty of Griffs to mail this microphone to the Hotel Management and how they would fit in the boardroom was a mastermind of Griffs because he knows Prossy, the head of the waitresses. She did precisely how she was told and got her share in cash. Whatever happened after that was not her concern, and she would get a job readily elsewhere through the influence of Griffs and his multiple contacts.

Nick eased himself from the window where he had hung for some time to observe his band of men.

Fully satisfied with the occupants of the room, he stepped on the ground again and checked the shotgun. It was skillfully okay. He glanced at his watch, and now it was five to 11.00 p.m. He began shaking instantly because the meeting was to end at 11.30p.m All along, there has been no explosion. Mr. Griffs wondered whether his gadget was old or not and if it was engaged, what else might fix it.

As time went on, there was no bhang or blow he could hear. Only left with four minutes to the closure of the meeting, he decided to do the inevitable.

Nick climbed onto the window again, and in position, he was able to view all those inside the house, and he could also hear the few final words of the boss of the gang.

"The society blames us for all the vengeful murders, rape, and kidnaps, but I would like to advise you to take extra security precautions. There are too many brutal killers around our hegemony. Any time, they can lay their hands on us. Again I would like to inform you that we shall devote $60,000 more to our cause and help defend our objectives". As he was about to take his seat, another man asked him a question.

"My election to a position in charge of information, and in my capacity, I would like you to explain how you solved the case I presented to you. That is the issue, which a hard-core criminal has penetrated our group curtains and is trying to lay us open." The man stopped.

Again the boss stood up," I made clear by saying be alert otherwise the more cash drawn as said earlier will be used for hiring more spies and bribing people especially the police to clear our records. He banged the table to strike home his point. At this juncture, Nick hardened his grip on the window with the left hand and with right; he raised the gun, finger on the trigger.

However, the delay was about a man bending and lowering over the table, resting both his hands. He could not rise immediately, so Nick weighed his chances of success and pulled the trigger; the man raised himself instantly as the trigger clicked, so the bullet got him in the chest instead of his head. He shuddered off balance and fell off before Nick could renew his aim; he got shot with three shots. This shooting incidence took Nick off the window like a lizard falling from a rooftop. He landed in the flower gardens and crawled as fast as he could into hiding. The gun in his hand was ready for any more prey. He cursed his failure. He regretted the absence of Walter and even compared words of misfortune that could have been uttered by Walter had he been there. He gathered his strength to put him in a better position to detect any shadows in the darker side of the compound. He ignored in pain.

The copper pieces got him in the head just close to the eyeballs, but there was no severe damage. It was some light cuts near the eyebrows. He congratulated himself for surviving this scene. There was a movement just a few yards away from him, and it was near the window where he had taken his aim from and got the hit back. He saw a man dressed in a black cloth move so fast past the rays of light that oozed through the broken glass. Before he could be aware of whom that was or whether he saw someone, he released some rapid shots in a sweeping angle, and all he heard was a groan and a shatter of bones as the man crumbled down heavily.

The groan of the man alerted the other men who were all out for the hunt. Nick remembered how risky his job had turned out to be; he even never understood before why the hotel appeared so vacant and no other public or private vehicles parked in the park yard at the early hours of the night. It was a proper booking for a purpose. Now that his prey had guns!

Nick heard a man crawl on all fours just so close to him on the left-hand side.

He stiffened and controlled his breath.

The suspicion that all the others have scattered out for a severe search, seeing his enemy draw nearer at a distance of about five meters, he let go some shots, which stopped the movement instantly, and there was no groan not crawls.

He waited further and realized no movements; he rolled towards the right, bringing him about fifteen meters to the fence. He heard someone say, "Ralph, can you hear that noise"? A man whose voice sounded so near about seven meters off asked?

"Could it be the winds?" The other man said instantly. Nick stopped like a cat. He waited for more noise to come. Judged their origins well and took a long aim by releasing some shots in that direction like a sprayer in a vegetable garden. There came a groan and some response of bullets from a Wesson and Smith Pistol. He shot more ammunition, and the gun sound faded so fast and realized that the guy might have received his sleeping pill and went fast asleep. He saw the first car cruise away without lights on. The second and then the third as if the birds were in disarray, and it was!

Nick waited for a few minutes and wanted to go, but the pain in his head restrained his efforts. He only thought of one thing to get away as fast as possible before the police surrounded the hotel since the gunshots were a signal enough...!

Nick vaulted himself over the fence, and he was out to freedom at last. Thus, the release of escaping danger Nick achieved, but still, ominous events ahead of him was a task yet to be precipitated by order of events. As he staggered around the lonely road at that hour nearing midnight, the crack in his head could not allow his legs to follow the traditional left and right; at times, he walked in circles and ended up in the same spot he had crossed. It was under such circumstances that Nicks' freedom still hung at abeyance.

Just as he was meandering along the road, a heavy motorcycle came screeching to a stop just a few meters ahead of him—no number plate.

"Come on by - hurry!" The cyclist commanded. Nicks' heart sunk into the abyss of his chest. His blood ran cold, and his breathing came in little gasps like that of a cat. He said nothing, nor did he think of shooting this bastard of a man.

"Nick just kept going; I'm Emmy!" Emmy had come down from the Motorcycle and carried Nick to the Motorcycle as the latter collapsed in shock and exhaustion, and bleeding he had encountered. He rode fast to a private clinic, where the wards are underground. It was a clinic used mainly by the secret service men, who wanted to keep away from government hospitals where most records are open.

Griffs had opened a billing account with the ABR clinic run by Dr. Ritchie and assisted by a Nurse called Brenda. He often paid cash in advance, for he knew his duty line, which came with unexpected injuries, accidents, and other dangerous consequences like brawls, fights, and torture. Nick is immediate to the clinic following his injuries.

But little did he know, neither did he know nor the people who carried him there. Because he was aware before he collapsed that his chances of reaching a hospital soon his own were next to impossibility.

Nick lay in the room, his left eye dressed and his head supported with two pillows.

He turned his head to the far side of the room and saw Brenda knitting a tablecloth. He didn't know exactly where he was or who this girl was. He tried to figure where he was, but his attempt died as the lady came to his aid.

"Nick, how do you feel now"?

"It's my skull; it's broken..."

"No, you have only sustained a light wound on the edge of your..."

She broke the sentence and sat on the edge of the bed, then continued,

"You need not worry, and it'll be okay." She assured him.

"How terrible...' Nick began and was interrupted by the lady,

"Don't blame yourself, Nick, not now...I love your courage and Strength,". She kissed his forehead, and he closed his eyes and slept.

Brenda had fallen in love with Nick at first sight, even when they were working on his wound with Dr. Ritchie; while Nick had not regained consciousness, she could not deny her strong feelings towards this patient. What is the detailed background of Brenda? Well, Brenda is unmarried, twenty-six of age. She had sought to be loved, married, and have a happy family. Still, no man seemed to come her way, maybe because she was dealing with halfhearted men who call themselves the fighters of justice, or was it an inborn omen that she should not fulfill the desires of heart regarding love? All these need to be sorted out by the powers above. Not did Dr. Ritchie show her affection other than the casual ward and theatre relationship, not even once. She lay there as "the untouched," not because she didn't want to be touched but solely because there was none to come by her side and sing praise for her affection.

She sat beside the bed admiring the man in his sleep, the rising and dropping of the chest and his somber calm face in his sleep. She looked at him not as a dangerous man but as a lonely and satisfying husband in all angles of humanity. Oh, wish.

After moments which seemed nearly an hour, he called her to the bedside and said," I want you to do a job for me." He kept quiet to wait for the points to strike her. Her eyes widened with surprise and confusion at the same time, for all her patients had been rough and hostile to handle, never did one request her for an exceptional hand; it was at times a tug of war to extract their names from them.

But this present seems to be the exact opposite of all those before.

"Oh yes, I'll do my best, and it's my pleasure to... She said lousily.

"Keep quiet about what has happened to my promise you will keep everything for yourself and no one else!" He sounded like a command, but Brenda got his words keenly.

Just when she left the room to go and prepare some coffee for the patient that is her customary duty, Nick picked the telephone receiver by the bedside and dialed Linda's number. Linda has been their company secretary since joining The Black Hawk alias Trap Music Studio and Video equipment sellers. It was an organization that specialized in selling even obscene tapes, war and crime films, and Music copyright infringements of all kinds. It had gained popularity among the locals since they looked at Black American Music as a rich cultural diversity. The majority of the people had been behind the International Crime scenes, with the influx of western ideology in dressing and star ways of social life; films provided an added classroom education through cinema halls and home videos.

The cinema education had enabled The Caliphs to amass a lot of money and their extra revenue from scandals and blackmail.

Linda was the secretary and computer operator in this company, Nick the Public relations officer cum spy. Linda had proved to be more of a helper than Nicks' imaginations could go. I'm not well, and remember not to shock the flies around by acting strange; it's all in your hands to do it for "Bye."

"Listen, boy..." The line went dead. "Gosh, he is in the pit again!" She mumbled.

Nick placed the receiver down hastily, and the door opened. He saw Brenda carry a thermos of coffee and a hot steaming pan of water. She placed the thermos on the table and the pan beside the bed. She picked the bottle of antiseptics from the chamber and got adhesives and lint for dressing the wound.

Slowly, she peeled the old plaster and managed the wound. There was a pre-condition for pus formation. She applied a bit of dry powder in the injury and dressed it nicely with a trained tenderness; Nick only moaned silent groans of men in the hands of women. Soon he laid comfortable sipping hot coffee to soothe his pains. The experience made him better by a hundredfold.

Brenda took this chance to break her professional ethics. After all, that is good artistry to a lonely and embittered woman; she thought as she crossed into Nick's territory.

All this happened as Nick was seeing, but he said no word. He was bemused beyond control, so much so that he lacked the guts to defend his separate ego.

Brenda sat right on the edge of the bed, where there was maximum body touch.

Nicks' thought about the previous events was fake. Now he could feel the nearness of Brenda and the heart that transported unmentioned sentences of togetherness.

The only thing Nick thought wise for the moment was to ask her to narrate the episode of his being in her house.

"You are in a private clinic, ward 4, room eight, and as for your coming here, I must begin by telling you who brought you here. Emmy, working under orders of his boss called Griffs, had an account here that always was prepaid. You were picked from a roadside on a motorcycle and brought you here when you were in comma". Nick began recollecting his memory to comprehend this story he was hearing, and it matched as far as the Motorcycle came by the roadside and stopped, who might have picked him was yet so faint to him at that time. Griffs was at this time in his life was experiencing some feelings of homesick and exhaustion.

Chapter 4

⌒⁊⁊⌒

MISDEMEANORS AND DECORUM EXPOSED THE JERRY SPRINGER SHOW WITH TWENTY FORMER PROSTITUTES

My story began with the lingering question about the American melting pot, the culture that has its meaning in various dimensions regarding the cultural amalgamation of new Americans from the different nationalities worldwide into the famous "American dream." Once again, Mr. Griffs makes another journey back to the USA as part of "Time Off" to visit one of his childhood friends in Detroit after spending adventurous time traveling to countries around the world. Here is Graff's story:

After accomplishing an exorbitant mission in South Africa, I decided to return to the USA, specifically Detroit. On the fateful morning of June 2000, at the turn of the Millennium, it was one of those fateful mornings while I had my breakfast; I picked a remote control from the coffee table and switched on the TV, and then flipped one channel after another. Here! Damn! I got the Jerry Springer Show and on the stage with Mr. Springer, was a medical doctor who came looking for his parents; despite his living in a foster home, he spoke about his achievements. He also acknowledged the fact that his biological parents were somewhere in the USA. He goes on to mention my name, "my father's name is called Mr. Griffins, who was once in New York City. He was the son of a wealthy man from Detroit who was once a runaway teenager. He and my Mom got into problems and got him kicked out of her apartment. She is called Susan Amanda. My Mom decided to put me into a foster care program because she was poor and couldn't maintain my upbringing, and so here I am. The captivated Jerry Springer show audience rattled the showroom with a round of applause in unison as a sign of appreciation for his achievement despite all forms of ordeals he had to overcome in his childhood. "I'm proud of you doctor for your great achievement from all odds life had thrown at you since, childhood" Jerry Springer acknowledged.

The Jerry Springer Show continued interviewing him, but I got shocked with disbelief. While the show continued, I recollected my past life vividly, kept wondering and overwhelmed by feelings of remorse.

Suddenly, I was struck by emotional pain and shouted three times very loud: Susan Amanda! Susan Amanda! Susan Amanda! Eh! Hey! Floods of rivers of tears ran down my chicks down to my chin. So, there are good things that can come out of prostitutes…? I wondered. It was a poignant testimony from my son, who has made a resurrection to my dead hopes. His demeanor was excellently flustered with more confidence, a professional by character. I stood up, cleared my face off streams of tears and went to the mirror, and checked myself in, reflecting the mirage of my past life filled with dangerous adventures. However, I decided to search for the Jerry Springer Show hotline telephone number or address, filled with trepidation. I, fortunately, found the hotline phone number enlisted in a telephone directory. While the interview with doctor Williams Griffins was ongoing, I called the Jerry Springer hotline and an audition to verify whether or not I was Mr. Griffins, as I claimed.

Dampen by the rendition of my call with the unfounded claim of fatherhood, the Jerry Springer audience was confused, as Jerry Springer's frowns through his spectacles and a sense of emotional grip expressed by his looks, which were stunned by the caller. A strong feeling of rugged emotional grip lingered around, holding the audience hostages and the presenter, Mr. Springer, in suspense. "Tell me! Are you insinuatingly telling us that this gentleman is a professional doctor and a general surgeon at the John Hopkins Hospital, your son? Are you one of that crazy EEERR! UMM! Out there trying to take advantage of a situation?" Jerry Springer inquired.

No, Certainly Not! Not wanting to take advantage of a situation. Sir! I beg your pardon for my humbleness and again humble myself to prove myself as the father of doctor Williams. Please arrange, and I will come to meet my son. "OK. I will do that for the sake of this poor and innocent soul." Jerry Springer replied. Why do you call him poor, sir? I inquired. "I called him poor because he has suffered from the dysfunctional familial poverty of parental love and care," Jerry responded. Oh! I see I broke down in tears and cried aloud. "Why are you crying when we have not confirmed this is indeed your son?" Jerry interrupted. Sir, I am calling because it is too deep for me to handle.

My heart is heavily fraught for losing my family. "OK, I see, take it easy, my friend," Jerry Springer replied.

We are not working deviously to deter people from expressing their grievances. So, I will ask Doctor Bill Griffins' permission first before allowing you to come and meet him. "Thank you, sir," I replied. OK, wait for a few seconds, and I will get back to you. There was a piece of ongoing music for keeping on hold a client. ♫♫♪

After a few minutes of waiting on the phone, the gentleman said they would send a special agent to come and take me to the show the following morning. I gave them my address, and excitedly, but anxiously too, I couldn't wait for the nightfall and daybreak. In the evening, I went to the nearest bar and ordered a glass of MacMohans to knock me down quickly so that I could wake up fresh the following day. Thus, I sipped and guzzled mouth-full after mouth-full of the whisky and ordered a special salad cocktail of superfoods with about fifteen ingredients, including fruits: baby spinach, cucumber, lettuces and tomatoes, feta cheese, curdled yogurt, slices of jalapeno, olives, Tuna, smoked beef, and beef lovers. I devoured the well-dressed salads and left as soon as possible before I could get too intoxicated to walk away.

I arrived in good timing and went straight to my bed and slept until morning. I woke up surprisingly at 6:30 am without a hangover and rushed to shower. After a shower, I made and ate my breakfast, which included: two scrambled eggs, sausages, bread plated with butter, and jam with a cup of decaffeinated coffee. At around 8:30 am, I heard a knock at the door. "Who is that?" I asked.

"We are Jerry Springer's agents." I went to the door and opened the door.

"Good morning, welcome; come in and have some coffee with me." I offered them coffee, but they were quick to say, "We are needed there at 10:00 am so, please dress up so that we go." Alright, "I will do what you have asked me to do." So, I rushed to my bedroom and dressed up. Then we left for the show.

At the Jerry Springer Show Room

We arrived in time, at around 9:45 am, and they gave us the front seats where guests were seated. Another show was going on, and people were arguing using obnoxious languages, and I could feel the filth right under my skin. The ambivalent showroom is rife with a profanely carefree mix of booing groups of people. Suddenly, I saw a scuffle that ensued between cheating boyfriends and girlfriends, followed by the: Bing! Bing! Bing! Bing! Bing! The bell rings as though there was a boxing tournament bell ringing at the Boxing or Wrestling Championship. I felt uncomfortable at first but gradually got used to the drama of hearing the stories of people coming up with their grievances. Some came in with high uncontrolled emotions accompanied by bashing and often interrupted by fist fighting.

Then, an elegantly dressed up and well-polished gentleman appeared who came in with some well-dressed up escort. The gentleman sat a few meters away from me. Then Jerry Springer began introducing the gentleman to the audience and the so-called caricatured crazy phony astute man that claimed to be the father. "Sorry, I'm not being rude here, but we have to be very diligent and smart today," Jerry warned.

Ah, hem! The well-groomed gentleman that was preparing himself to receive the man claiming to be his father gently said, "please, Mr.

Jerry, you never know... in my profession, we treat everybody with dignity."

So, Jerry asked me to identify myself. I sighed heavily and thought for a while with my head bowed down to recollect my bitter past and begin the story succinctly because many years have passed and recollection of the details was quite painful.

Yes, Sir, My name is Griffins Williams, the son of one of the wealthiest men in Detroit. My father had a big business in real estate, and he made a good fortune. One day, I read from the Holy Bible, the story of the prodigal son, and I thought it could play well with me, but when I asked my father for a share of his wealth because I knew I was the next heir to inherit, I was the next heir his wealth when he is gone. However, my demand amounted to nothing but a tragedy, hmmm, tragedy, indeed tragedy, nodding my head. What was the tragedy? Could you expound on that further? Jerry Springer interrupted.

My demand turned to a brutal brawl and resulted in a scuffle. My father took a hammer from his garage toolbox and wanted to hit me on the head, so I ran away and never returned. I was so obstinate, so much so that I decided to take refuge in New York City.

In New York City, life was tough and challenging regarding rents and finding a stable resident where I could live sustainably, but I managed well, though in crooked manners. I went to bars and met with ordinary women, some of who could accept me for a night or two. Then one evening, I met one beautiful lady who was so gorgeous but with a threatening beauty. She was well polished and dressed up. She was calm and responded with elegance. I approached her, and she was receptive. I engaged her in a few conversations and discovered she was out for a lookout for someone for the night or something even better. So, I introduced myself sincerely and without reservations. She was very attentive and decided to dismiss my stories. She said, "I came here to have a happy time, don't bore me with sad stories." Then, I switched to a moving subject. How I fell in love with one beautiful lady from a wealthy family, but though she loved me to the core, her parents were rude enough to get me tossed out.

The beautiful lady laughed intently, and she stretched her hand towards me and shook my hand to introduce herself "Susan Amanda" OK. Thank you, "Griffins William, but simply call me Griffs."

"I see. I'm offering you a bottle of beer, would you mind? Amanda asked. "No, Miss, thank you." I shied away. "Come on, don't be shy." Amanda joked. OK. I will take your offer. You are beautiful, and I cannot disappoint you for your generosity. "It's fine, Griffs my pleasure…." Amanda replied with a smile.

We sipped from glasses of red wine and dinned together. It was an excellent encounter with Susan that evening. We switched from one topic to another. We talked about Social Mobility, Social Stratification, the Echelon of New York City, and What Augments do the social fabric of this great but expensive City of the world offer, or what could one achieve from it?

Well, time to go home, and Susan asked me to accompany her. I thought for a while about how she could trust a stranger like me. "What are you thinking?" Amanda inquired when she noticed my silence and was absorbed in deep thought. "You know, I believe in you because you were honest from the beginning and your story reminded me of something serious in my early childhood," Amanda said. We went together to her apartment, and she asked me whether I had anywhere to spend the night. And I said, "No! I don't." she offered me her bed to sleep on for the night, and she slept on the couch that night.

The following morning, Amanda gave me a clean towel, toothpaste, and toothbrush for cleaning up in the bathroom. She prepared for both of us breakfast, and we ate breakfast together. I noticed her looking straight into my eyes without saying a word from across the other side of the table while eating her breakfast, but I lowered down my face in shyness. Then she gave me a sweet smile. Her eyes were glowing like a blue ocean with twinkles of sparkling lights of stars reflected in them. I was at first scared, and then I smiled back and said to her, you are gorgeous, and you scare me with your beauty. She laughed with enticing body language and smiled again. This time, she was hot, and she came and held my hand and kissed my hand. I was aroused to my peak and couldn't believe myself getting involved with a beautiful lady that I once got threatened to break my feelings about her. One thing led to another, and soon we were embracing each other with uncontrolled kisses. She held my hand and led me to the bedroom, and we had a great time… "You mean you had…" oops! Jerry exclaimed in an interruption. The crowd at the show busted into hysterical laughter. "Shhhhh! Quiet! Let's continue with the story." Jerry demanded.

Yes, and that was how she got pregnant that one time with me. So, she asked me to stay with her and do some chores for her in the apartment. However, one day Amanda went out into the City, and in her return, she came with one of her girlfriends, who was also gorgeous. Amanda introduced me to her as her boyfriend and then narrated how we met and how humble I was, Oh! Lucky you!..." Roslyn Betty shouted in excitement. OK. Now, I will leave you here to chat with him while I do some shopping at the grocery stores. I will be back in about 30 minutes.

"That's fine, we will wait for you." Roslyn said. Then Amanda left. There was music playing in the background from the FM radio station and the song was "Save the Last Dance for Me", a song sang by Michael Bublé:

♪♫. You can dance-every dance with the guy	If he asks if you're all alone
Who gives you the eye, let him hold you tight	Can he walk you home, you must tell him no
You can smile-every smile for the man	'Cause don't forget who's taking you home
Who held your hand neath the pale moon light	And in whose arms you're gonna be
But don't forget who's takin' you home	So darling, save the last dance for me
And in whose arms you're gonna be	Oh I know that the music's fine
So darlin' save the last dance for me	Like sparklin' wine, go and have your fun
Oh I know that the musics fine	Laugh and sing, but while we're apart
Like sparklin' wine, go and have your fun	Don't give your heart to anyone
Laugh and sing, but while we're apart	So don't forget who's taking you home

Don't give your heart to anyone	Or in who's arms you're gonna be
But don't forget who's takin' you home	So darling save the last dance for me
And in whose arms you're gonna be	So don't forget who's taking you home
So darlin' save the last dance for me	Or in who's arms you're gonna be
Baby don't you know I love you so	So darling save the last dance for me
Can't you feel it when we touch	Oh baby, won't you save the last dance for me
I will never never let you go	Ooh, you make a promise
I love you oh so much	That you'll save the last dance for me
You can dance, go and carry on	Save the last dance
Till the night is gone	The very last dance
And it's time to go	For me" 🎵🎵

Roslyn began looking at my eyes very intensely from across the living room while squeezing her thighs together momentarily, as though she was controlling something sweet and unbearable. Still, I was shy to look into her eyes. She sweetly smiled at me and said, "Why do you fear women's eyes? Are you afraid of women?" "No, I'm not," I replied. "Then what's wrong with me? Don't you like me?" "No, no, of course not...." I answered in confusion. She came closer and gave me a gentle kiss with searching eyes all over my face, but I was afraid that Amanda could be back in a few minutes and find me doing such a stupid thing with her friend. Ms. Roslyn came towards me and asked me to dance with her. When I stood up and signaled that I was ready to receive her offer, she immediately stretched out her hands and embraced me tightly at my waist while pressing her pubic region hard on mine. We danced chick-to-chick and felt each other's warmth. She then stuck out her tongue to carouse my earlobe and breathed close to my right ear while pressing her chick tightly on mine. I was getting warmed up and confused by the tactical romance that was heavily loaded with seduction.

Then, least did I expect Roslyn began touching my private parts, and right there! My genital sprang up, and I wasn't shy this time because of the arousal; nothing could stop me. My heart was racing due to excitement. Immediately, she said, honey ", you can make me wet if you can please; I love your shyness, baby"...she then got me on top of her and put me into her. Within 10 minutes, we got over the excitement, but I felt I should go again because she was irresistible. The heat in her was different from that of Amanda. She made a plan and said that she needed to have more of me for tonight. Then I answered her, "how possible could that be?"

She then said that she knew how. Amanda came in, and it was about one hour since she left.

Roslyn sat far as though nothing had happened. Then she said, "Amanda, I'm having my night shift tonight, but I lost my keys. Could you let Mr. Griffs come and sleep in my apartment for tonight and in the morning when I come back, and then I can drop him off?" "Yes, my friend, that's a good plan," said Amanda. "However, I need to ask his permission to do so." "Honey, are you willing to go and spend a night at Roslyn's tonight because she is going to work overnight and also because she lost her keys? There is no one to stay in her apartment when she is gone for her night shift" Yes, indeed, it's genuine to have someone take care of her apartment, so I can do that for her for tonight, honey. I answered.

Roslyn smiled and came towards me, and hugged me. While hugging me, she made sure she pressed her pubic center hard on mine. "What a kind heart you are," she commented.

The evening came, Roslyn picked me up, and we drove right to her apartment building. This surprising tactic took me by storm for it was smoothly executed. So, we had night-long orgies with many orgasms, and in the morning, both of us were still feeling very tired. A phone rang, and Roslyn picked the receiver and answered. "Yes, I just got in, and your gentleman has been so good to me. I will drop him off tonight when I have rested well." "OK, that's fine with me," Amanda answered. "May I say hi to him?" Amanda asked. Sure! Here is a phone for you, Mr. Griffs. Who is the person? I asked. "It's Amanda; she wants to say hi to you." Ms. Roslyn responded. "Hi, honey...yes, it was a good night...Love you bye."

We spent the whole day sleeping, and when evening came, Roslyn called Amanda that her boss had called an hour ago and asked her to go for another shift because the person on duty for the night had called sick. So, please, may I borrow your man again for the night? "That's fine with me," answered Amanda. "Can I say hi to him?" Sure! Roselyn handed the phone receiver, and we spoke lovingly, and she said that "she missed me a lot" Me too. "Love you," "Love you." Bye.

Roslyn cuddled with me throughout the day while sleeping. At around 3:30 pm, we went to the washroom and showered together in a walk-in Jacuzzi. Roslyn made an excellent noodle soup with some aphrodisiac ingredients, and we all got warmed up again. We were back on the heat in the bed and made passionate love with a bunch of orgasms. So, we all were tired and slept well throughout the night. When I was sober enough, I felt as though I was a merchandise for two women who got me into such confusions and disorientation as to whom among them I should dedicate myself in giving a hundred percent of my heart and love. They were both beautifully charming and elegant in executing decisions.

Moreover, in the following evening, I was dropped off by Roslyn, who promised with a declaration that: "any time she is available, just for me and no other men, period!"

I felt exhausted due to the two days of an exhaustive sexual encounter as a sex machine and sex manic spoiled notorious boy. I had to lick my wounds because of the exhaustion I was enduring for the night. Amanda was just there, ready for me in bed. I excused myself by saying that "I was experiencing a very excruciating pain in my back due to bad position while sleeping on the couch at Rosyln's apartment." "OK, that's understandable, honey," Amanda replied.

Early in the morning, Amanda woke up and began vomiting in the bathroom sink the following day. I inquired as to whether she was sick. Amanda said that "she was feeling feverish, nauseated and that I could escort her to the nearest clinic." We went to the nearest clinic and got her checked for any signs of food poisoning; the lab technician did urine and blood tests concurrently. The doctor called Amanda into his room, and soon I was called in too. Amanda gave me a sweet kiss, and the doctor congratulated me. I was surprised at the two actions and emotions towards me.

Then I inquired what it was all about. The doctor then broke the news, "your fiancée is pregnant, and she is not sick anyways, but you both should be calm with each other since this is your first experience, as couples."

My eyes filled with tears of joy. I kissed Amanda with genuine compassion and love. I sat on a higher chair and let Amanda sit on my thigh as though she was my baby. "I Love you so much that you never know how I adored you. Remember when I was timid and intimidated by your beauty?" Amanda laughed loud and said, "Doctor, this is my one-time hunt, and it was a successful hunt." The doctor also joined in the laughter. The doctor prescribed Amanda some vitamins and a few tablets to take while she was in her first trimester.

We went home and stayed together for two months. Then a phone call rang early in one morning at around 7:30 am, and the call was from Roslyn. "Good morning, and I hope everything is fine. Are you alright?" Amanda asked. Then, a few conversations went on and got serious. I could see the discomfort on Amanda's face. I grew weary at the sadden change of mood from Amanda.

Amanda hung up the phone with a bang! She came straight to me and asked me to explain myself to her. What happened? I asked. "Don't fool me, OK?" "Don't fool me, OK?" "Be truthful and let us settle this amicably, OK?" she warned.

Yes, please, I beg your pardon; help me to understand what's going on right now. "So you have been cheating at my back with Roslyn? Eh? Tell me right now or else…."

"Yes, please, honey," I pleaded. "Eeh!-Eeh! Shhh! No! Don't honey me; you are a cheat!" The exasperated Amanda vindicated. "I will recount sequentially to avoid misunderstandings…" "I'm listening." Amanda retorted. "Your friend Roslyn seduced me into loving her since the very first day you introduced me to her immediately after you left for groceries; she made me sleep with her on the coach here. Then she tricked you for having lost her apartment keys to take me to her apartment so that we could sleep with her throughout that night and the following night too". So, at that very moment until today, my mind is disturbed. Whether or not conscious, I feel deluded, and my conscience keeps flogging me for guilt, when in actual sense, my tender heart, I gave you hundred percent, yet the hawk swooped down from the sky and snatched from you a golden heart. My heart, you took it all. I felt lucid virgin boy who wasn't circumcised from things of this world, but being circumcised by wickedness now, the iniquity in me that cultivates lust. Will you forgive me?" I pleaded with Amanda. Amanda was in tears and sobbing heavily. I went and comforted her and joined her in tears. How could my best friend do such a thing to me? How, how? Amanda wept profoundly, and I kept pleading, I'm sorry, I genuinely love you; if not, I couldn't have recounted the whole story. "She is also pregnant for you," Amanda angrily shouted and burst into a more hysteric cry and wailing about how unfortunate she was since her parents divorced, and she thought she could at least trust a humble but loose man like Griffs.

I was overwhelmed by Amanda's emotional recollection of how deeply her past childhood trauma hurt her, and I fell in tears and cried even more than she wept because I remembered how kind she had been to me during the first day when we met while I was a stranger. Amanda began comforting me and admitted that I was the last man she had tried to choose for the rest of her life because many men just slept with her without being serious and humbled, in comparison with me.

Amanda and I continued living together, and I gave her my heart. In the ninth month, a baby boy was born. This baby boy was whom we named Williams Griffins. In the third year, another baby girl was born, and she was called Rose Amanda Griffins. However, on the other hand, Roslyn also gave birth to a baby boy and named him William Griffins. In another violation of my relationship with Amanda, Roslyn tricked me again, got pregnant, and moved out of the city to a distant town. Roslyn gave birth to a baby girl, and we named her Christine Amanda Griffins. This time she kept our relationship secret, but only asked me to visit the children on their birthdays.

Interjection

May I interject, Mr. Griffins? Jerry Springer inquired. Let me ask Dr. Williams Griffins whether he has any proof that relates to your story? Yes, sir! Would you please ask him?

"Dr. Williams Griffins, what could you tell us about this long and almost endless story from Mr. Griffins?" Jerry Springer inquired. Ahem! "Yes, all that Mr. Griffins has said seems to corroborate with the story my mother narrated to me; besides, it seems to be true, and yes, I have a sister named Rose Amanda Griffins. My mother is called Susan Amanda, and she has told me who my father is and what happened between him and her." Dr. Williams quantified the claims in sequences. May I ask him to come and shake your hands as a sign of reunion? Jerry asked. "Yes, please, sir." Dr. Williams answered.

Mr. Jerry Springer called my son and me to the front, and we hugged each other, and I broke into tears over my son's shoulder. "It's OK! It's OK! It's OK! Dad! It's OK!" "That's life, and now I'm a grown-up, a doctor at the John Hopkins Hospital, a practicing surgeon. And my sister is a judge at the New York Court." Dr. Williams consoled me.

I'm sorry, I pleaded with my son that I was unfortunate in my early life though I came from a wealthy family, my father's wealth, your grandfather, doesn't belong to me. My treasure is you and your sister with some of your siblings.

The whole room was captivated and mesmerized by our reunion. To our surprise, the rapture of our reunion resounded by several phone calls at the Jerry Springer Show hotline.

Our audience chanted a good father and good son! Good father and good son! And Jerry Springer, with an absorbingly concentrated frown on his face with a scowling gesture, called for our attention and calm. Shhhhh! "Breaking News! We have many women who want to see Mr. Griffs, and we have scheduled them for the meeting tomorrow", Jerry announced.

The Up Roar at the Jerry show

In the morning hours of the following day, twenty women showed up at the Jerry Springer Show, and they were familiar women I lived with during my crooked life in New York City. As a composed person, I least expected that the once hidden avalanches of former prostitutes who were into the game of survival were given audience by Jerry's show.

It was as though I accepted the offer of meeting them for massive confrontation at the request of Jerry Springer in the previous day and likened me to have accepted pressing on a classical keyboard of a piano that wrangled with melodies of bickering warlords. Moreover, when the ushers let the women into The Jerry Springer Show, immediately the room was filled with a problem of visibly angry and emotionally charged women who had stocked up their anger for many years of living frustrated lives. So, I felt like running away; for now, it was another defining moment of truths and shame. Whether or not to be called a nasty old failed man, I knew the women came in with vindictive moods.

The drama began with my reunion with Susan Amanda, but soon, the spoilers swooped in like vultures that have gathered to feast on the carcass of a dead buffalo after being wrestled down by a mighty lioness.

Each of these women came forward with hauls of insults and claims for child support, but I motioned to them that I had no relations with them at the time because they took care of me for just a night or two, and it was an only sexual pleasure they were looking for shallow satisfaction.

All women that came on the stage began insulting each other, and then one of them was peculiarly an old lady who came stooping with her Cane. When she opened her mouth, it was like a blast furnace for iron ore smelting was opened. She began speaking with a booming and crackling voice, but was occasionally interrupted by a thundering and rumbling cough. It seems she had chronic bronchitis. She shouted: "You cock suckers! You bitches! Shut up!... Coughing interrupted. "None of you knew how to take care of this handsome man who made good love to me all night long! He is my husband!" I noticed that she was the retiree that I had spent some months at her house and eloped with my girlfriend after asking my girlfriend to leave her home while visiting me and how we misbehaved with my girlfriend in her presence.

A scuffle ensued, and the stage for Jerry Show immediately filled with security guard bouncers for Jerry Springer Show. There was chaos, and the show was ongoing, but the audience cheered on for more of the scuffle to rise in temperatures, which could have escalated as explosive as a volcanic eruption.

Some of the women attacked the old lady who had a cane in her hand, but she fended them off by beating them off using the aluminum cane in her hand. She was very much alive with her deadly mouth, insulting and beating any woman that approached her. Bring it on! Bring it on! Come on, let's do it! You cock sucker! Bang! She then hits one lady on the forehead, and there is an ooze of blood from the gap of an open wound on her face. "Any bitch, who wants me to recreate their faces, let them come, and I will show them who the hell I am, cock suckers!" This warning came with peevish laughter. "I'm going to do your go damn thing, which other men didn't do well for you with this Cane...God damn it!" The old lady cautioned, meaning that she could deform any lady's face by hitting on their face with the aluminum cane and sarcastically using the Cane for making love to the women. This incidence of confusion among the women proved very dangerous because someone could sustain a terrible injury. So, I had to preen myself at this juncture and search for the right words to contain the situation rather than escalate the already volatile situation.

Jerry! Jerry! Jerry! Jerry! The audience cheered on.

Jerry Springer asked the audience to keep quiet so that he could ask each one of the women to tell their sides of their stories. "But first of all, I must warn you again not to agitate this program by aggravated assaults." Jerry cautioned. "What did you come to do here, young lady?" Jerry asked. The "young lady" was sarcastic about calling the old lady who came to the show claiming that Mr. Griffs was her husband and dismissing all women for not being suitable for Mr. Griffs.

"Ahem! I came here to meet Mr. Griffs, who eloped with one useless lady who came to my home while Mr. Griffs lived with me. He is my husband." She claimed. "Are you sure?" Jerry Springer asked. "Yes," she answered. "When were you married to him?" Jerry inquired. "Hamm...Hamm, Hamm, um! Sorry, there was no marriage certificate." The old lady replied.

"Mum! You don't qualify to be called the wife of Mr. Griffs, and besides, you are very old even to come here to fight everyone for no apparent good reason." Jerry affirms. Ms. Monica sobbed and stooped away in disappointment or embarrassment.

The audience cheered on. "Next person, and please introduce yourself." Jerry cautioned.

Ms. Roslyn Betty raised her hand, and Jerry Springer asked her to introduce herself. "My name is Roslyn Betty, and I am here to apologize to my friend Susan Amanda for rubbing her the wrong way… way back then when she introduced to me her boyfriend." "And who is that boyfriend?" inquired Jerry Springer. "That gentleman we all came to see," responded Roslyn. "Ooh! I see. And what happened?" Jerry Springer asked.

"May I ask my friend to forgive me for offending her? I'm truly very sorry for having behaved the way I did to you. I was desperate and looking for a man at that time, and again I want to ask for your forgiveness. It was lust for your handsome man that was why I messed it up." Roslyn recounted and broke into tears with a sob of remorse.

"I also concealed more of what I did with him after that first offense. I had another pregnancy with him, and now the boy and girl are well. They are all professionals. The boy studied engineering and now working for the high-tech industry. He is married to a beautiful wife, and now I have grand, beautiful children from his wife. The girl studied medicine, a highly respected surgeon at Syracuse General Hospital, New York. She is also married to a fellow doctor, and they have four children. All their children have their grandfather's name, Griffins." Roslyn Betty bravely recounted.

"Hmmm…Mm…Mm…Isssss, OK! What could you say about this matter or rather confession Susan Amanda?" Jerry Springer inquired. "Well, I forgive you, my dear friend; you broke my heart, yet, now you mend my heart again for being truthful. We all fell for a handsome man we took advantage of, but he is truly for me. That was why even today, you could witness for yourself in the event of our reunion." Amanda reminded Roslyn. Also, I'm grateful to learn that I have a stepson and daughter who are professionals. These are the blessings that we were probably looking for but through mysterious scenarios. Thank you for being sincere. Roselyn and Amanda hugged each other as a sign of reconciliation. They both broke into tears, and Jerry came around them, then hugged both of them as a sign of consolation. "You both are brave women, and I'm proud of you. Take courage, and through what both of you have done today, we have learned that every difficult condition is not permanent. You have all moved on very well, young ladies." Jerry encouraged them.

The Confession of all

Having heard of the poignant stories and broken hearts being restored and healed, the rest of the women were stunned by the drama of the reunion of Mr. Griffins and Amanda Rose. When Roslyn confessed to Amanda for wrongdoing, their friendship got restored, resulting in the mass confession of the rest of the women.

A certain percentage of other women confessed that they were driven into prostitution because of substance abuse, joining wrong friends, and choosing immoral lifestyles. However, others claimed to have been products of broken marriages and hardships. Yet others claimed that they had broken hearts from their first lovers and never trusted men again because of sustaining broken hearts from previous relationships. Moreover, others claimed to have gotten battered in their previous relationships. In addition, others promised to step up revenge against those dirty men. "Which dirty men?" Jerry interjected. One of the fidgeting women shouted aloud, "those men who are damn users." She seems to have some hangover from a drug or alcohol. "I'm done with those useless men who keep lying and who take from women." What?! Jerry asked. "They take money from women and run away to date other women. I hate them," she retorted. "OK. We are here to listen to your pains, OK?" Jerry assured. "What will you do with our pains? She answered. Well, we will find ways of restoring your life somewhat. "I need a steady job and a roof over my head…." She said. "Exactly, that's what we want every one of you to achieve. Life is short". Jerry answered her.

A round of applause rattled and crackled the showroom for moments. The audience stood up in a show of respect to the confession of victimized women.

Counseling

A conduit, as a forum, was formed by the Jerry Springer Charity to counsel all the traumatized women that came to claim child support from Mr. Griffins. The meeting was a form of psychological healing, which enabled the homeless women to regain their consciousness and to exit the pains in their lives. We will counsel each of you who is still suffering from some psychological burdens that need rehabilitation as soon as possible. Would you all accept meeting professionals who will talk to each of you privately, and then we shall proceed to another level after your sessions?

Then a chorus of resounding "Yes" from the audience raptured, followed by another round of applause from the audience, which lasted for two minutes. In respect to the initiative, all audiences stood up, showing respect to the enterprise.

Chapter 5

BACK TO THE MAIN TOPIC

After we administered good treatment on you, the Samaritan, who identified himself as Emmy, left and promised to check on you anytime. He promised that "he was first reporting important issues to his boss." She stopped. Nick's jaws dropped by hearing the utterance, "Important issues to his boss," it kept ringing in his brain over and over again. He checked his sides, no gun! "Could that be the issue"?

He thought. He knew as far as his intelligence could offer that Emmy had been the Good Samaritan in the story, and he was the one who had snatched his gun, and no wonder he had reported to Griffs the entire ordeal. That was it, yeah, that was it!

"No nonsense group of gangs." He mumbled to himself.

Brenda fell silent on realizing that the story she revealed had a grievous impact on the patient.

"Stop worrying yourself, Nick; you are in good hands"! She tried to soothe him.

"I am not worrying. I'm just wondering what could have happened had this Good Samaritan not come to my aid."

"Thank good heavens you are a lucky man! He expressed happiness to distract his thinking further and to make him feel relaxed. Sometimes, I fear some men who come here. They are often brutal and somewhat speechless. It makes life rather unpleasing to keep running this private clinic though it helps them a lot. But it's only today that I have got a patient who can listen attentively and answer reasonably! That means a lot" this was all Nick said for the moment.

"Yeah, it means a lot; I had an uncle who was once a musician for and badly enough, and he joined a business of kidnapping young girls. We could investigate those girls used as sex slaves in underground establishments such as brothels to find residents of their agents. He was netted in late 1989 and charged for several counts of offenses that led to a verdict to imprison him for 120 months with hard labor and a colossal fine of 10,000 dollars.

The problem is to date; is that we cannot trace his whereabouts". After the narratives, one of the sex slave girls stopped sadly, and a few painful tears rolled down her cheeks.

Nick, who had been passionate all his life, had to wave the tears away. He was both saddened and fascinated by the story. He said, "It happens to the best of us!" Brenda turned to look at him.

It was right here that they heard the doorbell ring. The brothel members were not aware of the heavy engine of the land cruiser outside.

Brenda excused herself and rushed to the door. She saw a strange woman, a young lady with a deadly complexion of an assassin; small brown eyes that never swayed nor blinked anyhow kept them gazing at her intensely, which Brenda almost thought her last hour had come. The woman spoke just. "I want to see Nick, Madam."

"There is no one here called Nick."

Brenda managed to say through tight teeth. "Madam, I stopped kidding when I was ten years old. They say that he is here. Okay, go back to the house and tell him it's Linda who wants him!" she yelled at Brenda. The yelling caused a spin in her head, and she reached Nick's room, almost fainting. "What's the problem?" Nick was trying to raise himself from the coach. "A woman... Linda."

"She wants to see you," Brenda said. It is a kind of broken sentence that came out of Brenda's mouth.

"Oh, that girl… it's okay… Don't be scared. Let her come in". Nick commanded her; she rushed immediately to avoid causing an unfavorable scene.

Linda came into the house immediately and went straight to Nick. Nick offered to greet her, and she took his hand firmly and gripped them for some time. She asked him right off", why did you delay?" Knowing that had Nick been on the alert, he would not have earned what he had now. He pointed to the chair by the bedside, and Linda sat down.

"Please, it was… hard. Especially the angle," Nick managed to say. At this time, Brenda excused herself and left the room. Linda took a long look at her behind till the door was closed after her.

"I don't like that woman!" Linda declared

"She's good and caring," Nick confirmed. Linda is the type of person who does not go with second thoughts when she points a gun at you. That makes Nick fear her very much, especially when Linda is annoyed. She sat with her legs kept a pace though it exposed her thighs a great deal. Her bag lay on her lap. She wore dark glasses on her head and her well-maintained hair into a dark floppy mane that she attached into one with a pin. She dressed in a short-tight jeans skirt, and a loose purple blouse and a green neck scarf were there in its proper place.

She wore no earrings that day, and she was in a pair of sneaker boots. She had frowned on entering the room, and when she saw Nick, she felt like jumping to hug him, but she managed to control her shock.

"How have you managed to come so fast?

"I was here in Johannesburg. When you telephoned me in Pot Elizabeth, my sister spoke and immediately rang me here in Johannesburg. I rushed up and down, and I recalled having bumped into a man called Griffs, and he helped me out; I'm here". She explained.

"I never knew you have a sister or she could talk like you; that's wonderful!"

"Sometimes, it's hard to believe." Linda said, "You could have..." Her statement went dry. She lashed open her bag and lit a stick of cigarette. Nick retook this opportunity to narrate his episode, and Linda listened attentively while drawing a lungful of her smoldering cigar. At last, Nick said, "You'll do me a job for some extra pay and don't disown me; I trust your capability."

"But I...give me time to think". Linda cut short her statement.

"Then the bird will fly away! Listen, there is Secretary Alison of The Caliphs, and he is a partner in the proprietary of the Hotel lovelier, and that's why the meeting should have taken place there.

They knew which rooms had ears and which had none. So, what I want you to do is start calling there for this week and feed me with reports.

Remember Alison is so weak on ladies of your caliber, and he may ask you out for some company or probably a night in bed with him. Then this will provide you with a chance to drug him and I'll come in".

"Is that what you want me to do? Going to bed," Linda asked with anger behind her tone.

"Not that it's a possibility depending on how the circumstances may be and how you feel about it," Nick explained. "Alright, how or what drug am I supposed to administer on him? "It's easy. If you know the elementary skills of injecting a person, you will drive in him a good dose of succinylcholine. He'll be well packed, and I'll snatch him like a baby". Linda kept quiet and considered all that mass with her intelligence and weighed all the other side effects should anything go wrong. They sorted out the technical aspect of this job and the financial considerations in the form of money and any issues that needed clarifications.

"If the drug takes longer to work on him, you add him a bullet in the head or chest.

But what will happen here is that the bullet issue will arouse the attention of the hotel occupants. Think about that, please". Nick supplemented.

"I have a new 48 special with a silencer".

Linda affirmed.

54

"So far, so nice!" Nick agreed, at last; he eyed Linda benignly and waited for her response." "I see little chance for hope." Linda said."

"Leave chances to themselves, you do what is necessary, and chances will be on your side."

Nick continued.

"Then the money is not enough," Linda said dryly.

"Okay.

Twelve". Nick said.

"That's an insult!" Linda chipped in.

"Fifteen for the best" Nick spoke carefully to tune this girl into the final bait, and he touched his dressed wound lightly and feigned a sigh.

"That is a deal." She said insolently.

"I'm leaving, Nick." She announced her departure, but before Jackie could speak, Brenda appeared at the door,

"Would you like some tea or Coffee?" She stood ashamed as the lady paused to clear her mind from something but gave in at last.

"Some tea will be good. Thanks".

Linda glanced at her watch and reasserted herself to the hollow of the armchair. They sat all three in the room to sip coffee, served three on the round glass table. Brenda talked to Nick about his health, but Linda was not attentive since her mind was preoccupied with her big task ahead!

Linda had suffered from severe depression in her late teens, especially at nineteen when she was addicted to Cocaine and Marijuana—constantly feeling rejected and yet avid for love. As things were not equal on her side, she derived other ways of life so contrary to everyday life.

At twenty, she spent in jail with charges such as smuggling opium into her high school, kidnap and rape of a seventeen-year-old Joel, and possessing a lethal weapon without a firearms certificate.

She had wandered across the World at one time as a prostitute and a call girl, another a secretary cam spy, and somewhere as a once married but unhappy woman. Now this new job of hers that she had massaged like a baby for nearly six years. All these experiences in life had taught her cruelty, and she had murdered a handful for money. She once swore to her associates during jokes that she cares less for her own life and others. This one fact made Nick fear her a great deal. At one point of intimacy, she once told Nick that she amassed wealth to own her house in Port Elizabeth by cajoling Mr. Ralph to support her claim for an ill-gotten wealth at the Bank. "You are so daring!" Nick had said. Many had loved her, but she gained no pleasure from them. During the party thrown for the member of Prime Health Solutions, a splinter agency of The Caliphs, when Nick gave her a lover's kiss in the banquet room after much boozing, the event ended with no repeat nor follow-ups.

Chapter 6

THE SUSPICIOUS ORGIES

Now she was in her living room, seated in the sofa, Linda raced her mind on the assignment offered by Nick. She stood up suddenly and walked aimlessly in the room but ended in her bedroom. Linda picked a small chit from under her pillow, now she dropped it as soon as the words sank into her subconscious mind. She kicked off her Canvas boots. Her blouse flew as she took it off and it landed on the bed. She went out into the bathroom and had a shower.

At dinner, her plate rested full in front of her. She sat peering into the face of Alison in a photo Nick had sent together with the chit. After a long duration, Linda collected her plates and went to the kitchen. She wasn't happy at least; the nausea that gyrated in her stomach had twisted her intestines into a very hard knot of fire that kept burning her groins on and on.

Later in her bedroom as she changed her clothing, Linda picked the phone and rang Nick's number in Griffs house at Jeff Mountains. "Hullo", His profound baritone echoed in her ears.

"I'm..." she began and changed her words slightly and then continued, "Begin timing!" She uttered these words as if they were farewell to him, she then hang up the phone. Linda was again seated in her room when she checked her pistol and found it was loaded. She didn't pick much paper except for her pistol and money that lay in the cool compartments of her handbag. She locked her door with a strange amount of care and went to her blue Renault that the housekeeper had packed at the front door and she was on her way - for man hunting.

The events of the night were less promising than she had anticipated. There were few customers in the bar and most seemed distracted from the others than usual. As she gauged her mind, she realized it might be the impact of the shoot out that occurred there recently. That night, she was in her room at 11:30p.m and promised her diary would contain some positive effects in the day to come. She went fast asleep as soon as her head hit the pillows and she was in the cool embrace of the sheets. It again became her routine to call there as Nick had advised but fortune seemed to escape her on the night of the seventh day. It was on this day that Alison picked on Linda.

"Madam good body, do your mind joining me in the bar?" His eyes narrowed so much that it implied he only expected an "unconditional yes". Sensing all this, Linda had to accept the offer. She gazed at him briefly but she was able to figure that he was cold and polite. She hid her face in the pages of the novel she was pretending to read.

"Brandy", he said to the waiter minutes later when Linda had joined him. He motioned Linda to order her favorite. She did and they were sipping together at the table. "They call me Alison, an auditor with the Supreme Accountants and Management Consultants. What is your names lady? He asked. "I'm Claudia, a clinical attendant with the Stay Fit Health Club". Linda said with equal mischief. In order to avoid speculations she knew very well that should any question arise concerning her profession, she would tackle them promptly and correctly. They chatted here and there about their work, tastes, likes and dislikes and hobbies. A chain of lies backed the only funny springboard here was that everyone lied. Who cares, they were both guarding their separate egos and personalities. It therefore mattered less especially to Linda, as she knew the true particulars of Alison and what he had so far said were a hundred percent lies except for his name that he sort of shortened. On the part of Alison, he believed all that Linda had said and thought she was one of those thousands of call girls and that was exactly what Linda wanted him to believe and good enough, it worked on his intelligence.

Up to this time, 11.45p.m, Nick had not yet popped in at the Bar. Linda began reconsidering her fate but life being both right and left and having experienced bitter sorrows herself, her heart had sunk beyond the usual depth of self-pity. She was ready for even the worst in life and that enabled her to sit there all this time with this god admit it of a man and she the seasoned prostitute for his night. She then began thinking why of all things on earth, a man is so eager to pour his wealth on a woman who in the end is either cheated or despised. Why did Nick expose her to this kind of torment knowing very well that is impact will be long.

Why did Alison pick her in the first place and what are there in his mind?

"Why do men just wish women could do they say and no more chance for her version of the situation."

Alison excused him and went to the Bar-counter to place orders for room service knowing that his girl had recoiled and wasn't going to be easy mingling her with people. She looked so astute and still very cute and captivating, her freshly washed hair looked so elegant and smashing. She applied a little make up and she did not wear her exotic clothes or sprayed exotic perfume on her body, but she had a little roll on and that was all. So it's better to go and provide her a warm company in his bedroom. He arrived at the table and announced proudly, "I'm usually early in bed madam. Would you please join me upstairs?" He walked to her side and picked her long brown jacket as she hyped the small Gucci bag on her slender shoulder. She walked close by his side not paying attention to the curious on lookers who kept following their steps with long leering looks on their faces and some of the ladies were seen giggling and murmuring to themselves. She abandoned all her previous thoughts and asked no question. He offered his hand and she slid her small arm easily. They disappeared into a wide corridor walking like newly found friends in silence. He tilted his head and wanted to plant a kiss on her forehead but she brushed him aside. At the door of Alison's private room down the corridor, he turned to her and took her in his arms.

"You are going to like this tonight, my little blonde!" He said into her ears and squeezed her into his large chest. It felt so nice to be this intimate to a man after a long time. Linda thought. "It'll be grateful to both of us". She said.

"I like the way you talk, nice girl". He kissed her passionately. His body was warm and he charmed her more when he opened his arms and wrapped them across her shoulder.

He was drooping over her and this created an extra sensation in him that could not be equaled by most of his previous encounters because Linda was much younger and better looking lady. Most of his bedfellows were some good years over age. He had got an early customer who was as if thirty four year old against his fifty-four whom he devoured casually. That night he really celebrated his catch. Tonight, he had Linda thirty-two but she looked younger than her age of about twenty seven, this calls for another celebration. He kissed her hard on the lips and Linda responded dearly and he enjoyed the connection a great deal. He began fondling her breasts and his hands rested a bit longer on the rose nipples that sent a highly electrifying ecstatic rundown her spine and it was drowning her out of breath. Then Alison disintegrated the closeness to get time to open the door. They entered in the spacious and well-furnished room. The light shone brightly and this fashioned the bizarre of colors that reached Linda's eyes.

"You have a nice room". She commented.

"Thank you". Alison said. They were seated in the cozy suite and sipping brandy and white wine. "Is it your type that you always talk less?" Alison asked.

"I spent my childhood mostly alone. There were not many young ones at home. This explains why I tend to talk less". She explained. "Then, you might have had rough time growing up. May I know how old you are? Alison continued.

"I'm thirty two". Linda replied.

"You look younger than that. On what good diet have you been maintaining yourself?" Alison asked.

"Ordinary meals, no special diet, I'm afraid my income does not allow for that". Linda said.

"That's surprising. I can't help myself look younger which ever ways". Alison said resignedly. After they had finished taking their drinks, Alison moved from his sofa to where Linda sat. He pressed his hands on her shoulders and kissed her tenderly. He started massaging her body.

He touched her inner thighs, which were made accessible due to the long slit of her short floral skirt. She was breathing heavily intentionally. With the other hand, he raised her blouse higher and kissed her nipples that stood almost erect instantly. As he continued to bring her to this sky limit of sensation, she on her part was groaning of excitement. The wine had started wearing down and all that was happening to her appeared as though she was watching a love film or dreaming about one. She never took seriously what was happening to her while she was giving herself willingly to the man.

"I didn't know if you are the type who wants to be hands off …" He said.

"I don't encourage…" Linda managed to say with difficulty.

"I am very grateful and extremely happy" Alison said, Pride in his eyes and desire behind his tone. She had realized that what she had initially anticipated as cool in bed had turned out to be a hot star yet to be proved.

Without giving her much time for thinking, he carried her off from the sofa and went with her to the bedroom. He laid her on the bed and he stripped himself nude. She almost lost her breath on seeing his hairy chest. He came to the bed and sat on the edge. He undressed her neatly like a mother peeling the wet towels and nappies off the baby. She has half nude save for her silken knickers. He kissed her nipples again and the mound swells greatly. At thirty-two, it was a blessing that Linda's breasts still maintained that upright stance.

"Will you take off the blouse" He said mumbled into her ears.

"Why Als?" Linda asked feeling dizzy.

"I love it if you did that yourself". He said.

Linda tried to say something but her words were choked as his tongue found its way into her mouth. Without any delay, he raised her gently and laid her on the bed and hooked his thumb around the elastic waistband, and the pant went down to her knees and heels and off. Now it came under the pillows. She was nude.

He eased himself a bit from the edge of the bed and was lying by her side. She tensed a little for fear of all that will happen to her.

She had not had sex for quite a long time and her body felt jelly like in his hands and she wondered her capacity to tolerate a real and lively romance and sex.

He took this chance to get on top of her. She felt crashed underneath his weight. He kissed her eyebrows and her nose then lastly his mouth was stuck to her month. Chewing her lips in little sensational biter It was this time that her tongue found its way into his mouth; just then it sounded signal enough thus he introduced his member right into the chasm that lay in between her thighs, "Slowly!" she whispered in his ears as the plug went into the depth of her being. "Easy, my body He assured her. As the plug reached its final destination he kept cool the act of ups and downs. He wanted the shivers of love to stop. Her brain turned automatically into a frenzied galaxy of affection for this man. She began wondering how this sexually ideal man should be destined to die. There would be a chain of women who would mourn his death for decades. She reconsidered Nick's hatred for this man and affirmed her deal was strictly for money which she badly needed. This was the fifteen thousand dollar contract she had entered into and this almost brought back all her sorrows in life.

Lucky God.

Alison began moving swiftly and Linda joined him in this play by tapping on his back with her thin slender fingers. They moved in bed for duration of about fifteen minutes and when the climax came, it got both of them almost off guard and sent their bodies into waver of passion. When the tremors stopped, he thanked her for the play and disengaged himself.

"It has have been marvelous," Linda whispered. They lay side by side to regain strength for another weary drill. That was the order of that night.

In the morning, Linda woke up to find her body muscles had become more relaxed than ever all these years of sexual boycott. Alison still snored heavily. The time was 5:45 a.m. Linda picked a gown from the wardrobe and went to shower. She was back in the room after ten minutes to find Alison was still sleeping. Last night she had played tactics to ensure that he slept before her and it worked now she was up before his eyes made contact with light.

She dressed in her clothes and applied little cream from his wardrobe to soothe her skin. She sat by the bedside chair and read a magazine that he had left on the table the previous evening. She got the hell of her life stories:

It contained the secret contacts of The Caliphs Organisation ranging from the top to the lowest and sensitive international allies.

The man started turning in bed and Linda had to put the book in its place within time lag of the blink of an eye.

He did not wake fully from his sleep nor did he take glance of any occurrence in the room. This gained Linda the additional second to put the book exactly how he had placed it.

Without wasting much time, she took off her blouse and started waking Alison. He opened his eyes and closed them immediately on seeing the light. Then he opened them again. He gazed at Linda and cleared his throat. "You are up early, baby?" He asked.

"Just a few minutes ago…Good morning Als". Linda said. "Good morning. Can you ring the reception for breakfast?" Alison asked.

"That will be a good idea. Thank you". Linda said, "What's the number?"

She asked. "Seven, five, four, two …" He spelt out slowly and dearly, Linda dialed quickly but what rang in her mind was that all numbers seemed to start with seven or end with the same figure. As the receptionist picked up the phone, she said hello and Linda handed the receiver to Alison. He covered the mouthpiece and asked Linda what she would like for breakfast. "Egg sandwich, fruit salads and coffee for two" He answered. He replaced the receiver on the cradle after singing their words in the phone. He spoke fluently and softly.

He came out of bed wrapped a towel around his waist, and went in the bathroom for a shower. Linda closed the bedroom door after him and came to sit by the bedside. She put back on her blouse and wanted to go through a few paragraphs in the magazine once more. Unfortunately, as she turned, she got another page instead of the previous page and what she got on this page was somewhat very necessary information.

"Number 7000 is for T.R Roberts, 7001 is for Warren Davidson and 7002 is for Alison Cook, 7003, is for Maxwell Osborn...

With a rush and temerity and double care, she replaced the book in its place and sat alert and tensionless. The door opened, Alison came in and as he tried to close it, the waitress shoved in her head with a trolley of breakfast.

"Good morning". The lady said as she served the two on the table. "Good morning", hang in the air as both Linda and Alison replied the greetings. The waitress left the room immediately after serving and she wore a beaming smile that Linda admired and hated out of jealousy at the same time. This gave time to Alison to dress up for breakfast.

They sat down together to take breakfast. Linda enjoyed salads and eggs most while Alison crashed sandwiches more eagerly. They talked less. "How was the night?" Alison had asked.

"So nice!" Linda replied.

"How I wish if we could replay the game on Saturday, two days from now," Alison said. "Why not on Sunday?" Linda asked.

"I don't think I will get time on Sunday! I'm afraid". Alison had said.

His face fell down and he was looking at the carpet not saying anything.

Linda had guessed right. If Saturday were scheduled for the reply, then he would not be there to see the morning of Sunday. Whether he had known about his death or he was talking by instinct remained a game of puzzle to be sorted out on Saturday night. Linda framed her mind that Nick should be around, that time to administer his wrath on this man.

After finishing breakfast, Alison got up and from the wardrobe, he removed his briefcase and in a few minutes it lay open on the bed. He picked the magazine that was on the table and placed it on top of the papers in his case. From the corner of the briefcases, he removed a bundle of Rand. Picked one thousand five hundred (1500 Rand) and gave to Linda, "This is your transport" He peeled two more thousands and gave her without saying a word. Linda got it that this was the charge for the night she had spent with him.

I'm going for a meeting down town, please". He announced. I'm as well on my own way "Linda informed, she left the room before him because he was yet packing some papers in his briefcase. But what propelled Linda to go so fast was that she never wanted to be seen walk in the company of Mr. Alison and that she had collected much information for Nick which she needed to relay to him at the fastest moment possible.

On reaching the pavement outside in front of the Hotel, she was able to wave a taxi to her temporary house in Spring Hotel. She wanted to change, apply some make up to her composure and then reach Nick's place in Jeff Highlands and deliver to him the message she had collected the night before.

Saturday was not a very clear day. The day was not so busy because of the cloudy atmosphere and light drizzles. Nick had been indoors for most of the time. He was fabricating plans for the big catch Alison. Griffs had suggested that he was sending Emmy to execute that deal. But Nick had maintained most of the news brought by Linda to him. He never appreciated the point that Emmy takes over from him but the mere fact that his head still ached was enough to convince him to lie in bed and let things happen under different hands for a change. All he needed to do was to alert Linda about this decision of Griffs so that she would be prepared for all that lay ahead.

"I don't encourage intruders in my field. But if he is coming as a spectator, that's fine!" Linda had tele - informed him as he rang her.

That evening, Linda dressed up with much care, she put on bras such that her boobs shook with every step she made and it aroused Alison beyond normal sexual encounters. Emmy was seated at the counter giving him a one hundred-percentage advantage to monitor all that happened in the house. He had swallowed several cans of coke but never had the guts for strong booze. He talked to no one. His face was set in a way as would reveal the intensity of his emotions. He had put in a heavy private Jacket with a Jean hat and Jean trousers.

At 11.45, Alison and Linda left the room Emmy had seen this happen. Linda and her man left the main exit and headed for a sub corridor. Emmy on his part passed through the patio and entered the rooms from the hindquarters.

At the door of Alison's private suite, he grabbed Linda by the waist and hugged her tenderly squeezing her bums thereby forcing her boobs to compress against his chest muscles. She closed in on him and they kissed. He began uttering a tantalizing massage about how sexy or not is her small body and she on her part rested her hands on his shoulders and the heat of the kiss spread throughout their bodies. As the passion reached the preliminary climax, he began ravaging around her small bottoms and then the valley between her things. As his hands went down the shapely flesh of her thighs, she tensed and his eyes turned wolf red. Horrors began! His eyes fixed on her face for a moment but all he wanted to see was what was clearly painted on her face, "Something lay in the cool pinnacle of her thighs, fastened with a bandage on it was her silencer pistol, this was what shocked them both".

Linda, well aware of the multitude of her danger, without any possible delay, the gun was in her hand aimed at him. He jerked her backwards both collapsing to the floor separately. Linda was quick to rise and added him another shot to make sure the job was done well. Alison collapsed into one funny heap in front of the door. She thought very fast to drag his body into a hiding but the last shot had shattered the window glass. This ushered in a platter of footsteps on the first floor that urged her out in the Tennis court three shots were sprayed after her and she showed her clean heels.

Again there was a shatter of windowpanes behind her and more shots. Linda ran as fast as she could, bending low. She released three shots in that direction for which the shots came and instantly, there was silence. This gave her yet another courage to race for the fence that seemed some ten meters off. But before she was midway, she stumbled and fell under the small trees, Linda rose and struggled on, this time, and the pursuers were so close after her. She raised her gun to shoot at them and only heard a clicking sound the gun was empty. One of the men shouted "Don't move!" Linda stopped in front of them like a rabbit trapped in the headlamps of a car. She wanted to jump on them but these two men were distantly placed that the other could take a bitter charge at her. They were pointing their guns ruthlessly at her. "Drop your weapon!!" Shouted the other... She obeyed them and quickly like waving off a fly.

Emmy appeared from behind the two men and took good care of them each with two pieces of copper so expertly that there was extended oblivion of silence. Linda once more was in the briskly wings of hope and freedom with Emmy as the captain in a flight to safe haven.

That was the first phase of elimination of The Caliphs Organisation members, Nick was so pleased to hear the news that night but what kept hiking in his mind was the mere chance that a third or fourth pair of ears might have heard.

This unpredictable riddle was solved the following morning as Nick read the Newspapers and confirmed that the assassins were still at large and no eyewitness reports were available. That was the confusion wanted to continue to be heard over the city of Johannesburg. And the last Train to Kimberly was able to swap Linda into yet another enclaves of runners' away- "escapees". So far so good!

That day in the dawn hours, Nick had to board a C130 plane to a secret landing found in the Southern Dry lands of Botswana at Chikwalakwala and there he found his land of peace in the company of his Black Warriors. Once more, life seemed on rails.

Chapter 7

⁓

THE PASSPORTS

In the early days of August 2002, Nick had recovered totally from the effects of his previous ordeals. There was not even a spot of blemish on his face. Nick dyed his hair a little and acquired two more passports under different names and nationalities. One was a South African and the other of Botswana. All these were possible through the help of his concubine, one called Sheila. Sheila had an uncle working in the immigration and Passport office, and the latter had a friend in the foreign office. Therefore, all these opportunities enabled Nick to amass travel documents to cross-vast boundaries without any single spot of suspicion. This time Nick was given yet another deal. This time a crucial mission of stealing some information believed to be the Master files of The Caliphs Organisation.

Nick hired a small tourist land rover with camping gears on the carrier for a short safari expedition to Kruger national park. He drove the dusty Kalahari roads alone in the heat of the car. Nick's cartons of packed food in the hind packing space never aroused his appetite. All he had in the lonely mileage was a pack of glucose with coke cans to wash it down.

As he reached the small shanty suburbs of Lobatse town in the touchline of South African Periphery, he had to call down for a light meal. The restaurant attendants servedNick with smoked fish in Okra broth and some steamed Irish potatoes and egg rolls.

From here, he added an extra meal of Irish stew with a Boom Barger that entered his food flask. Then he drove on down to the main roads that led to Mafeking.

Following Nick's long drive and struggling with the steering wheel for all that long, he had to retire for a nap in the courtyards of Crystal Lords Hotel in the town of Kimberley.

As he reached Cape Town after a day's drive, mainly using the hilly and valley roads, he had to pack at last at a lonesome beach on the parts of the west of the town. Here, he ate his Boom Barger stew mix and relapsed in his tent to sip a bottle of dry gin to kill the exhaustion that seemed to be burning his muscles still.

Getting tipsy, he had to sleep for the night, and that was three days to the D-hours of his mission.

In the big mansion at Cape Complex, on floor twelve, which houses the offices of the undersecretary of The Caliphs Organisation, Nick heaved himself through the lift's doors and entered the main room of the reception. The young little Tsonga girl at the desk smiled at him.

He beamed a broad gin, almost uncovering his roving desire for the light brown African girls he had longed to go to bed with him. "Can I help you?"

"I want to see Mr. Gad Levison, Madam."

"He's out of office Sir, Can you leave a message?"

"This is business. I must see Mr. Levison personally!" He sounded like a command, and his deep voice trailed with power. "Maybe you come back later if you can..."

"That's not possible; show me into his office; it's an urgent matter." He snarled at the young black girl.

"Okay, Sir, but you'll have to wait in the visitors' lounge," she affirmed.

"I'm supposed to leave Cape Town in a few hours, and I was on appointment." She dashed out the appointment book and rapped through the list in a groovy speed and at last raised her head to say," What's your name, sir?"

"I'm Onan O'Brian." Soon her eyes were in the book, and again she raised her head to look at him, "They booked you for 2.30p.m, if you can wait for fifteen more minutes, please. Nick said no word this time, but his hands reached the breast pocket of his coat, and he pulled out a neat bundle of used Rand notes.

He peeled for her a 50R note; within no time, Nick walks into the blue-curtained and well-furnished office of Mr. Levison.

Seated behind a big oak table was Mr. Levison, whose beaming smile broadened as he saw his visitor. "Well done, Mr. Onan, well done, it has been long."

"True, it has been long, Mr. Levison. How are you?" Nick asked. Mr. Levison waved him to a seat, saying, "Please do sit down, mister, I...Maud, some coffee for two". He shouted to the Secretary. The small girl spun around and nearly raced to go and pick the thermos from the Canteen. Nick gets a little opportunity to talk about an imaginary business with Mr. Levison. "We are expecting some more parcels of leopard skins from your boys, but since long, no consignment has reached our base in Dallas, U.S.A. So our Special Agent and Director have sent me to talk that out with you and seek alternative goods if, at all you can avail them, we are losing millions in the offshore business, and there is a need to close this gap of wires that end on wrong hands".

"That mishap resulted from the untimely death of a top Jewish man, Mr. Alison got shot by a lady who masked her face and was untraceable anywhere before we lost four men in a shootout in one of the small hotels in Johannesburg. All these have slackened our operations, and now we are living on the fence".

"We sent some monetary equivalent of those goods, and now our business in the fancy clothes factory has dwindled below the bottom of the graph, and we fear that we are soon running out of business."

"That far we are together..." Maud popped in with two glasses and a golden flask and served them. She retired into her room immediately and never came back to interrupt the tough talks of her boss. "We are sending you some fifty sheets of the spotted skin by road because all the significant customs outlets have increased their security equipment and chances of sneaking like a flash of lightning are entirely bleak! Levison said.

"How will that work out then?" Nick asked. "We shall have to weld that lot underneath one of our cars sealed in a flat sheet of iron, which can be slit open during offloading and packing onto hired cargo liner we shall arrange. That arrangement has already taken a good direction, but only that we are short of money due to the problems we experienced over last year and increased personal security for all our agents! "Then that way, I agree we are still partners or if you let us down, and then no more deal." As Nick said this, his left hand was in the trouser pocket, and with the right, he offered Levison a final touch of painful greeting in a gesture of a satanic handshake. As Levison was descending to sit on his rolling chair, Nick shot at him three balls, two in the chest, one in the center of his face, and Levison dropped like an apple that had gone right from the tree.

Nick checked in the desk drawer for any secret book or diary and found the keys to the computer room. He unlocked the door at a speed of a hawk, but he struggled to remove the top of the desktop computer. Levinson released a CD from the DVD Rom and the extra master copier to clean the computer memory. He had to remove the battery; searching further, and he found a brown file containing a pack of confidential documents that Levison scooped tacked into the inner pockets of his coat. He left the room with that majesty of a personality only matched by the Sheriff's Department, Private Detectives.

Compact with all that he came to sweep, he emerged in the main reception and waved a "simple bye" to the receptionist, who seemed busy and preoccupied with a heap of papers. With the tender patience of her profession, she first managed to say, "Bye, Mister, see you again." However, she never even bothered to raise her head to see that this man was or his identity.

Nick was already behind the wheel and driving fast to the Museum of African problems in the township of Carlersburg. The highway was clear and so pressing on the gas peddles caused to adjust the speed beyond the maximum that Nick's foot rested flat, and the heavy engine land rover almost seemed like a small bucket afloat a river. He was racing at 150 km/h when suddenly a police siren disturbed his ears. He was on the main road rightly from Cape Town, and at this particular instance, there was no hope for diversion, and then he drove on.

At a small roundabout, just before he could think of turning his car around, there was a roadblock by a chain of police vehicles. Luckily when he visited Levison, Nick was in an old hired Volkswagen. However, still driving in a Landrover of Kalahari Tours and Travel Agency, he seemed nearly a perfect Tourist. These actions prove that the two gentlemen were good at disguising themselves as tourists.

Further, chance being on his side during the travel, he had set ablaze a passport of Mr. Onan Brian. The good news was that the pack of passports stamped with visas in the names of Eric Mohgarden were intact. Nick placed the remaining tickets in the inner breast pocket of his heavy jacket. The Suit he had put on when visiting Mr. Levison was total ash miles behind.

He stopped the Rover vehicle at the road held up, and shoved his head through the window to greet the police officer, "Good evening, sir" "Good evening, May I see your identity papers, please! "The man spoke heavy Xhosa accent, and Nick, having known at least many local languages in South Africa, was able to tell from which part of the country the Policeman came. After examining the passport, visa, and car hiring documents of Eric Mohgarden, he said at last, 'We have a problem down in Cape, and we have been tracking some long hours back, and the said killers are nowhere, "Sorry, I wish you, well officers." Nick had to say, and as he received his documents, he drove on and away from the scene of trouble and past West Bean Fort.

Reaching Galesburg, Nick realized that he was overtaxing his nerves, as a matter of compromise according to Biological estimates; he had to return the hired car to an agent of Kalahari Tours and Travel based in Salisbury. He booked himself a room in a Hotel Motel in the hub of the town and spent the night in sleepless and fitful dreaming nightmares.

Early the following day, the 25th of June 2003, Nick boarded a small public taxi and started his retreat to the secret enclave in Botswana, where he lived freely like a bird in the sky. They reached Kimberley, refilled the oil, added some gas to the car, and drove on. By mere fateful incidence, he forgot to buy the morning papers of the Sunday Times, but the gloomy rings of death seemed to hang on him as the driver switched on the car radio and the news broadcast came online.

The South News at One:

"...Mr. Levison and outstanding under Secretary of a car Sales Agency has been shot dead in his office. The murderer claimed to be a business guru and wanted to meet the deceased on personal business issues. However, the Secretary's office reports say that the assassin identified himself as Onan O'Brian - Afro American; his true particulars are of necessity for establishment.

However, investigations are still..."

Nick's heart sank into the great depression of his chest cavity, and the looks in his eyes were far more ghostly than ordinary. The driver adjusted the rearview mirror and glanced at Nick but said nothing.

Nick waited for all his courage to gather, and when they reached a few miles to the township of Warrenton, he waved the driver to stop, and he disembarked.

Walking on the sidewalk, he reached a newspaper vendor and bought copies of the day's papers and went to seat himself at an open pub and ordered a pair of sausages and a bottle of water.

He kept gazing at the photo of Mr. Levison, now dead, that kept lingering on the front page of the paper. He read in a quick way the details so far unearthed about the murder and counseled himself that as far as the reports were concerned, there was no single evidence as would drag him to the handrails of the police cells.

But the only obstacle to his liberty was the Secretary, Miss. Maud. The only task left to clean the trail of reports and investigations is to clear out with Maud. Nick thought sadly. Miss Maud, maybe, could be handled by Linda. The trek of his mental escapade stopped!

In a small rented house at Cradock, Mr. T.R Roberts lay on relaxing on a rocking chair reading the evening papers. Ice cream and siphon by his side on a table and an old cowboy hat on his head.

His darkened face almost seemed so grave. The spectacle he wore almost sag to the lower end of his nose. He kept gazing into the writings on the paper and a portrait face of the deceased Mr. Levison. His ego and plans all seemed to be clashing against time and secrecy.

But what mattered to him most was the telephone call from Miss. Maud that the computer records were inconsistent. It was the core issue that touched his nerves greatly.

Mr. Roberts knew from then on; their secret codes had altered numbers. What kept perturbing his brain was the degree of accuracy in interpreting the code and the personal safety of all the remaining members of The Black Hawk.

Mr. Roberts is a stranger to any of the members personally, except Warren Davidson, Alison Cook now dead, and Maxwell Osborn. Late Levison never even saw eyes with him. But at least all those working in the Cape Town Office knew his private telephone number, and they could alert him in cases of danger. Mr. Warren gave this number, and he had said that it belongs to T.J Morris, and that's how those who contacted Roberts on telephone knew him to be; Mr. Morris where he works or lives and any further particulars, not known. The numbers were secret commands given by Warren as a last resort in case of danger happening to any of the members.

There was no single opportunity where Mr. Roberts did not attend any of the Organisation's meetings, nor did he engage in physical activities of the groups. The man on the charge was Mr. Warren, but the Master Mind was Mr. Roberts, a Multi-Million Dollar boss. He owned a chain of hotels and restaurants in the major towns of South Africa, all registered under different names and managed by several other hands. Still, all the profits go into separate accounts within and outside South Africa.

Mr. Roberts married in his early twenties and divorced some eight years later. He had a son called Phillip, now studying by correspondence with United European Detective High School and a full-time student with the Kings College London, Faculty of War Studies. The divorced lady Rose now earns an annual income of 20,000$ on top of rental payments and medical bills from her former husband as a private arrangement to keep her silent about the true personality of Mr. Roberts. In her late sixties, she lives a strange life in a small village in Bophuthatswana. She maintains a daily habit of recording in her diary, which she hopes to hand over to her son Phillip as her last present to him or if Phillip turns twenty-five, which is just six years to come.

Roberts lives a secluded life because he was born to a polygamous father. In such a complex environment, Roberts lived a needy behavior and received marginally more diminutive than most of his peers. He went to low-grade schools and often fell sort of his basic needs.

As an ambition, he had it that he wanted to be a prosperous businessman, and this encouraged him to read a lot of books to broaden his mind about the other sides of life and the world in general.

He had started smoking by fifteen. By seventeen, he was sunk fully into a boozers club; somehow, he managed to complete both junior and general school certificates before enrolling for a law course in criminology. He got involved in petty crimes and later robbed an agent carrying a parcel of gold tablets in milk bottles, and he killed the man; to date, no arrests made.

At this time, Roberts jumped out of home and started a mafia-type of life in Kimberley and entered into the real estate business, but this was short-lived and mixed this with robberies and errands on seas. He would sneak in Maputo and work as a fuel clerk with some guys loading crude oil on Ocean Vessels, a job he very much liked because it was lucrative and exposed him a great deal to guys who connected to many offshore networks. Now he is what he wanted to be. Not even his son knows the true history of the family. All he knows is that his mother married another man. He often joked that "Each family for itself but God for us all, and the devil makes the grave of the hind most much deeper!"

At exactly 6.45p.m, Roberts entered his bedroom, picked a private telephone, and talked to Warren and Osborn. He informed them to meet him in Middleburg, and that was all he had said. After emptying two scotch whiskey glasses, he dressed in his usual brown trousers, a spotted shirt, a jacket, and jungle boots topped with gray fat and dark glasses, and he entered the garage to drive in his Limousin.

At Middleburg, Maud was the first to arrive, as is typical with her character, followed by Warren and Osborn, who came by a time difference of thirty minutes, respectively. As the Limousin appeared at the gate, Mr. Ronnie promptly opened the gates and drove the black Limousin to the parking yard. Mr. Roberts emerged from the drivers' side and walked in silence to the entrance of the big mansion.

His face was well curved with a low-maintained mustache, and he commanded a high power level. It was Mr. Warren who greeted him first, "Welcome, Mr. Morris, sorry for all the mishaps." He stopped with a dry face.

"Done, boy!" Roberts said. He paced to the far end of the living room and seated himself on an office chair next to a drawing table. Mr. Maud and Osborn pledged allegiance to the man behind all the drive and the one who had offered them a livelihood.

"I'm a bit put down with the Misfortune that has befallen us. But don't give up the struggle is my Motto". Roberts announced. He gave no time for any preliminary talks nor asked questions.

He seemed well packed with information and the needed money to buy the way. Warren and Osborn were quiet, and Maud took this chance to go to the kitchen and fetch some coffee for them all. The look in the face of the three men was far cloudier than an obscene era recorded to a partnership. The whole room went cold and seemed automatically chilly, and gravy likes a holocaust cemetery.

The woman was already considering improvements as the boss had shadowy corners of his memory; he knew that a trap with a snare was around them, and somehow, any day, anytime, anything could happen to them.

While Osborn, who was once a game ranger and having wandered the world both in good seasons and bad situations and being a personal slave of sedatives, felt more relaxed.

Maud came back with a thermos and a tray with four cups. She served them and retreated with her cup to a small chair by the fireplace and kept herself busy by rekindling the heat.

"Warren, tomorrow first thing in the morning, write cheques worth 10,000 Rand per head to all members of my clique and ensure that they acquire fresh passports under new names. We live in the wrong land, but if anyone can succeed, I would prefer you get passports from the neighboring countries. You know how that line goes with the help of our disguised members abroad. Add figure three to all our code, and the word "no help" should be the last signal in our dangerous calls. A day mentioned in a phone call means three days later, destroy all documentary evidence of our company, knowing the records are in our heads very well. "I will create a buffer zone to safeguard in case of any security disruption during this dangerous mission." It is a means to get very well away and lost forever!" he sipped coffee from his cup and rested it on to the table, and resumed his briefing to the top officials, the ones who were each pin and tablet of the organization.

"Mr. Osborn, you did very well. One more thing, get to know who is betraying us. Miss Maud, leave South Africa by next evening and go to Zimbabwe, I have a private house there, and I know I can contact you. Any questions?" he stopped tensely and looked at each person with that patience of godmother nursing a baby to the breast milk. The three kept gazing at him agape with billion treks of questions: how did he know or that much? How has he planned all that in the nick of time? How sure is he about success? How did he know the contacts he talked to very well? Why did he not give them a chance to speak first place e? Why did he not conceal his identity? How and why did he manage to talk calmly and in cold breath despite the dreadful ordeals? …

The trend of questions kept ringing in the minds of the three as the boss talked at last: now, I'm gone take care!"

Roberts rose from his seat and left the half-empty cup on the table; he walked casually to the door, and a few minutes later, the Limousin drove away. That was the beginning of a dangerous move and yet the painfully last moment for The Caliphs Organisation, and by midnight, the other members had gone their ways.

Chapter 8

⌒◆⌒

THE SECRET OF THE CALIPH DOSSIERS AND COVERT OPERATIONS

Nick was back in his house in Messina in the far north of the country. He sat in the living room with a brown envelope containing a dozen photos of his accomplished targets while Roselyn was in the kitchen preparing some lunch. Nick peeped into the plain wall to gather his thoughts but the bad sides seemed to crash on him. He tried to think about Linda and all he summed up was "A lunatic!" Of late, Nick had acknowledged that Linda was capable of generosity and yet equally volatile as concerns quarrels and misunderstandings. As his thoughts grew wider and a heap, he jerked as the phone rang "Hello! He said into the mouthpiece after picking the receiver "Is that your Ja?" A woman's voice was heard and distinguished as one belonging to Linda. He eased himself in the hollow of the sofa as he said, "Honey something amiss Linda's voice, "Nope. Mr. Griffs called here this morning and wanted to see you, Can I... She searched for the right ward and continued, "Where are you now?'

"Somewhere...somehow" This was their secret code that signals danger and urgency. Both ended the calls on either side. Nick drove in his Celica as fast as he could that he was in Petersburg within a few hours. Reaching the hub of Johannesburg, he hurried his turn to the road that led to the township of Mafeking. It was 4:50 p.m. when he at last made it to the boarders of Botswana and South Africa. There was little delay at the customs checkpoint as he had his papers in order. By 6:38 p.m. he had made it to Lobatse and was heading to the Jeff highlands to meet his friend, Mr. Griffs. The house appeared so desolate like a deserted hospital!

Almost no lights were seen except in the living room. As usual, the gate was flung open with that utmost welcome spirit, but the events that ensued never seemed to match this either. He stopped the engine as the car drew close to the parked Golf GTI. He was out and walking t the main door

Emmy was there to open for them and painfully, here was no word uttered between them. He passed and got himself near the round tea table. Griffs was on the far side seated on an armchair. As Nick's eyes moved about in a wave of reach for a third person, he turned to look at Emmy who was locking the door and adding the chains.

As their eyes met, Emmy raised his shoulders in a shrug and Nick had to divert his attention to Griffs who seemed equally, locked and tart.

It's good that you are in time and in one shape "Griffs started. He picked a stick from his pack of cigarettes and lit it.

Smoking leisurely, he resumed his narration to Nick.

Bad news, Joan has gone missing for two days. All our efforts to file in details about her destiny are totally fruitless. Now there seems to be a reason behind, her kidnap. As you may already guess, it seems we are all under some snoopy injection and the doses are beginning to get at our nerves ". He stopped to drag on his cigar. Emmy took this chance to seat him and poured some coffee for them all.

He waved his left hand towards the ceiling and sipped onto his cup of coffee and then puffed a bit. From the inner pocket of his jacket, he removed a blue covered note book and handed it to Jackie, saying, "Read this, my dear, it has the source and turmoil's of my brain, which were known to me only but now I would wish you get a share of it and if you can't appreciate it now, please preserve the message in your brain, for anytime any day and anyhow, it will be useful to you and you 'II help save us from this evil domination."

He stopped sadly and with the back of his left hands he wiped off a few drops of tears that threatened to blur his vision. As Nick moved closer to pick the book from his hands which he released with ease, he said, "when I laugh, it doesn't come from deep down the bottom of my heart but it's reminisce of humanity that I have to bear a smile. I have never learnt patience and love in my life; I believed in: "I don't know what it means to be good because I've seen many bad things done and I don't know what it means to be bad because I've seen good things done - then I don't know what it means to be anything!"

Nick was shivering with the weighty comments and it almost took him all his grandeur to open the first leaf of the booklet, now old and yellowish with age and repeated handling! From the first frontal page, it was labeled, "The long dreadful memories of the lives they have left behind!" He read silently.

The verses shocking were about a future deadly disease that affects the blood and is caused by mutation due to radioactive exposure. The revelation portrayed that the blood from victims would turn milky and thick due to impairments of the key cells. The most affected will be the white cells and plasma hence he had named the future disease in his own notes as "Plasma" for he had no medical or scientific terminology equivalent at the present time. This was a deliberate multiplication of induced mutation disorder fabricated from the labs by cruel staff that lived on dirty wealth and cared less because all they knew was money! They had manufactured several defective lenses that cause eye cataract, night blindness among others.

Millions of lives will be lost before a team of Doctors would to sit down and device a vaccine and a possible drug. This factor of the revelation which was dug from a dossier of The Caliphs had altered his brain a great deal because the Aids Pandemic has caused a terrific challenge to mankind affecting millions in Africa and Asia. It has often left him wide awake most of the hours and he got fitful nights.

Nick had to blink several time stop a drop of tears from his eyes and yet his eyes has a full pool of water and lazily he cleaned then and placed the book on the heavy teak table. Once more, there was silence. The night birds took this to share the shrill of their songs and the echoes from the nearby bushes and hillsides reached the house where the men sat and when the owl took its turn, the noise was not only killing but also heart freezing.

Now Emmy who had not said any word all that long cleared his throat and said,

"Some more Coffee please"

"That will be appreciated brother!" Griffs said. This was his first time to say the word brother to Emmy or even to most of his acquaintances - who are male.

Emmy fetched a steaming kettle from the coal stove and poured its content in three porcelain cups. He went back to the Kitchen and he fetched a tray of dry roasted meat. They all started eating and sipping of coffee in silence and at half past midnight, they went to sleep in separate rooms.

At six in the morning, they were all seated at the dining table and had breakfast together. Minutes later, they went down to the plans each had formulated overnight for their "Operation Rescue". It was Griffs who chaired the meeting.

"In my view, Jackie should leave present house and move out of that country and that applies to Linda too. Clean all your bank accounts by withdrawals or transfer of funds to new accounts under different names elsewhere.

Sweep your houses clean of any useful materials and rent them off to new people. Within a month, you'll have to sell your car or get a new registration log of a neighboring country. We shall have to man our operations from remote operations from remote control up to maturity of our contract with you". He stopped, giving time to Jackie to say his side of the story.

"We need a small microchip reader to access data I snatched from The Caliphs headquarters. Devise a means of tracing the personalities behind this organization and find out where Joan is whether dead or alive. Other words you had said are up to terms with my plan". He was quiet - Nick.

"The issue of Joan I will handle by myself. I predict they will not kill her nor have they done any grievous harm to her except some threats and minor bodily damage to make her vomit the secrets about us. To cut off the trail of information, I'm about to set off on my errand and I want that doubt sorted out by sunrise tomorrow. I need some 15.00R for my adventures - boss". Emmy stopped, his head tilted towards the right and his eyes sagged into their sockets making him appear much skinny and drained than before. His lips were set in a flat slip and yet his voice much steady and compassionate. Griffs considered the viability of these remarks and after a moments pause, he said, "Some ten thousand will buy your way through and this time, you should know, you are moving along with all our enemies determined to lay hands on you should that chance avail itself - I' am giving you a set of time able explosives, You know when to apply them".

Mr. Griffs disappeared into his private room and this gave chance to Emmy and Nick to talk briefly.

"You are sure she's alive and held captive? Nick asked, his voice crocky.

"I wouldn't say that or if she was killed, her body would be dropped somewhere and the papers would not miss to publish an article carrying messages about tattered female body along whatever road and the supposed killers whether arrested or at large. So leave that to me, and my last advice to you is that, please do talk less or ask a few questions only because I personally, I don't think I am willing to give many answers whatsoever" He was tense. Nick kept quiet for nothing that he was in a boat with highly stiff navigator. To keep the status quo and maintain an atmosphere of assured peace, he said no further words.

Griffs had arrived with a metallic box in his hands. Reaching the table he lay the toolbox down and opened it. In it were tubes of explosive, and detonators and he picked the ones he wanted and gave them to Emmy with a brief explanation about the operational skills and precautions?

At 10.45a.m, they separated. Griffs remained in the house, Nick drove to Gaberone to catch a plane to Pietersburg and Emmy rode on his high-powered seal motorcycle.

Two days later, Emmy was in Pearl, a growing township neighbouring the tangle skein semi capital of Cape Town. He was in a small night camping Restaurant. After submerging his spirits with some Gin, he had dosed early that night and by 3.00a.m, he was wide-awake.

He switched on the bedside lamp and read through the pages of Joan's memoir. There was nothing of importance nor was there anything he could fully comprehend and do some follow up. There were lists of telephone numbers but no names. Joan had little or only a few words scribed in her book.

Emmy probed his mind yet further and at 5.00 am he had to send Griffs yet another call - both saying "so far no light", Griffs only replied both calls with a chuckle and that meant a lot to them. After asserting himself the futility of his job and whatever became of Joan, at 5.45 am, he started an endless stampede of ringing all those members.

He was standing in a public booth; his car packed a few meters away. The bag of explosives so tenderly welded at the car suspension, a good metallic sheet enclosed it. He waited after the dial for whomever to pick up the phone. The first was through, the second was picked but when he missed the right words, it was replaced as fast as it was picked, the third number went through," Joanna..." was all he said. There was a moment's delay at the other side and a cocky male voice, "What about her?"

"She wants to speak to you..." he was cold and shivered after saying those words. "Speak to whom?" the other man shouted.

"You" Emmy affirmed.

"I don't think she knows me or I know her".

"That you'll sort out later, Ok...?" Emmy said.

"Then you are on a wrong number."

"She gave it to me". Emmy said and regretted having said this - for if she were held captive, it would speed up her torture or hasten her death - he thought sadly. Coming out of the booth he had to run faster to enter behind the wheel of his borrowed car.

He sped the care as fast and by the early morning hours at 8.50a.m, he was in Cape Town. All along his brain had been sketching the ugly part of this errand, the time had gone dead just as he had planned to say yet one more word. It had made him freeze and hung up with the "going".

On reaching the main post office, he parked the car neatly and raced the flight of steps till he was in line with the other customers who had brought in mails or came to fetch their parcels. As he reached the large counter he said," Excuse me, the telephone Directory please? The cool Tshona girl acted with that grace of Florence Nightingale and he moved aside to let the others have their way to the small glass slot.

As he checked the numbers from top to bottom across, he realized there was only one which matched with those in the notebook - he put a small star besides it in the note book and versus that, he wrote the names of the book to the Tshona girl and out he raced back to his car and developed traffic madness once his feet rested on the pedals. The wheels almost left a screech but long time experience made him balance that before any louder noise could be heard. He was heading onto the highway from Cape to Pretoria. The great North road - as it was called some time.

Driving past Pearl, he soon reached the small township of Worcester and he drove right to the left as he met the road that led to "Just Garage". Military factory and the house of a Motor Tycoon - Quarcoo-his closest advisor and the Good Samaritan who had lent him a second hand Datsun but in a good running condition.

Seated in the small office behind a big mahogany desk was Davis Quarcoo. The man beamed on seeing Emmy back in one peace. They talked briefly about what so far had been uncovered and Mr. Davis took this chance to elaborate on plans netting this lady Maisey. That her house is in Kroonstad. From his secret papers, she was killed in 1986 but her postal address remained unchanged.

The man now living in the house bought if from her mother and he is a highly wanted police suspect. He stood charges of car robbery but escaped spot free to Zimbabwe until the security waters had stopped boiling. It was so difficult to interdict him because from that year till late, there was no intergovernmental cooperation on matters concerning security around the Southern African States. It was a taboo to exchange state records of crime coupled with inconsistency and bribery that dwindled the full operations of the watchdog down the tip of Africa and under such circumstances. Many state enemies had emerged winners in a game where there was no referee! That was how the killer of Maisy dogged and fooled the world around and managed to come and buy the house some three years later and now lived in it as a freeman.

The two men added their side of the story together and realized later that the man could be a highly placed servant of the block mind Organisation. As the pieces of information began falling together, Mr. David remembered he had an order for repairs on a Motor vehicle - he ditched his order and traced the particulars; Log number SU14329X, the man who paid the charges was Steve Maharijan half Indian, half African. What were so peculiar about this order were the special demands. The man requested a gear cog of a tractor be fitted on to the gearbox of a Volkswagen beetle - the effect was an added speed and increased power of the gears and all these were expected complete by a time lapse of four hours. David had worked so hard to please his customer - As he checked the date of the order, it was 14th July 1986, just a few months before Maisy was predicted dead. This could have been the car for the mission, he thought sadly.

"Then you need to drive to the town council offices of Kroonstad and get to know the house number and its present occupants. By night fall you can ring me and we shall work on whatever turns out -together so I'm in line with you for 5000R tonight - Bye!" He stopped.

Mr. David went back to his work of designing a Car bomb that is to be fixed onto the coiled spring of a car. Should there be any compression enough to squeeze the wire foliage, the circuit would be complete and the explosion would occur. The bomb consisted of a simple beer can, two poles of magnesium rod - multi stripes of magnesium ribbons and nitrite compounds. These were sealed in the can and the two rods were wired on a DC adapter. The last equipment was wired on to the lines of care wiring system. Two other ends were entangled separately and these would be glued or cello taped on the car spring and any compression or contraction would switch on an electric current, which would be multiplied by the adapter, and the ribbons with the help of the nitrite would blaze. The technical theory was that the bomb be fitted close to the fuel tank and any little blaze would set riot to the tank and the whole car will be in flames! Had tested the first sample of the bomb and it proved effective within seventy five seconds after ignition and the heat and flame was capable of ravaging a car fuel tank. Wonderful trick!

He had murmured to himself. If events later proved to be worth trying, he had better be prepared from upstairs to the roots.

He was back in his private metal drawing room. He had properly finished welding the fuel lines on to a 200-litre drum and the task left was to fit this drum in the car and finish with the last connections. He removed the rear seats of his Nissan Patrol and he heaved this huge drum in its place. Working so carefully, he attached some supporting bars of pipe and checking with all his muscular power, the drum was so intact and well fitting.

He then refilled it to the brim and the fuel lines were joined to those of the original factory design. To make an extra camouflage, he had to weld a large sheet on the secret tank added some synthetic sheet on top of it that it appeared almost like it was from the car designers themselves and lastly, he had to spread fabric sheep skin for additional pretext of luxury.

That was step number II.

The speed governor, he pulled completely down and the acceleration line, he manipulated in a way that the original spring and level system, he removed totally. He fitted a dual level system such that any light force pressed on the accelerator pedal will mean 175% of the usual speed!

"It is a criminal offence if you do come within personal distance to me but when you get hit and hurt, it is not my fault. The question that killed who bothers me less once I'm behind the wheels of a car of my own mechanism.

Before he left the workshop to go back to his office, he fixed there a thirty-metre piece of Magnesium ribbon under the drives seat.

He had sat behind the large table for nearly an hour or more and what he was thinking was so colossal that when the telephone rang, it almost took him unawares. Hello! He snarled into the mouthpiece.

"Hi it's me show boy!" Emmy said.
"Then re-examine your brain". Emmy said,
"That will mean you'll mean you'll talk not".
Davis "No matter but your head is vital capital for your life!" Emmy assured.

Their last two statements meant "Davis had been working so hard for the past few hours that he is presently resting and Emmy had said that understood, he should keep resting in one place obviously the office up to when he came back with the news.

"Thanks for feeling so warm at least". Davis said.
"It's my pleasure to be that way my dear". Emmy responded. They both placed the receivers and once more, the wings of hell were loose.

Emmy arrived slightly after seven in the evening and met Davis in the Garage office where they exchanged a few words. "With green lights established to land…?" Emmy said jokingly once he was in the soft cushions of the office sofa.

"I hope the passenger isn't scared with takeoffs and landings! Was all that David said? "The books indicate that Mr. Steve Maharijan is still the one who paid all utilities including electricity and water. This was detected by forensic evidence of reading and interpreting his signatures characterized by large S&M symbols. Further it was reviewed by the signature specialist that the samples were almost as good as believed but the one million question was why Steve became the true occupant while the first owner in the house registry book had not signed any transfer forms and worse still the files of Maisy Orlando were found missing."

This confusion would have been solved by the State Investigation Agency, but South Africa being a corrupt and confused nation, many of these questions would be swept under the carpet without answers, no one bothers who's who and who did what unless the fire was glowing or burning right under their feet.

Emmy and Davis took this as their noble obligation to bring to light or fate the personality behind this dilemma and the killing of Maisy.

After supper that night, the two drove to a small Hotel Oscar Rendezvous in Kroonstad and had a few cans of beer as nursing aid to their troubled minds. They had emptied at least three cans per person when Mr. Steve dropped in with young nice looking girls. They walked the small passage till they were seated in a corner.

Emmy had heard a heavy engine of a short chassis land rover a few minutes before the couple surfaced in the Hotel. But they had made no signs of notifying his colleague. The new arrivals were served a majesty pack of gentility and were now siphoning their drinks through straws.

Mr. Steve was dressed in a brown Travelling shirt and added a gray coat and green trousers while his date was in denim and a polo neck. Her blue sweater was no her shoulders. She had her hair set in curls and there was one floppy that hovered around the middle her face and gave her an increased air of charms. When she smiled, her nose pointed sharply and her teeth showed a perfection of dental formula when the fine thin lips parted. She had lovely dimples which killed Steven's heart and he craved to die smiling between her things. That was why a man of his character moved with these slender Shona girls.

All this while, they were talking in low baritones to avoid eavesdropping by any other guests in the bar. Emmy in great moods already picking clues about what they would tackle incase the plans went right.

More cans went down their throats and the other couple went spooning dishes of chicken chips and salads in chili sources. As time went by, Emmy and Davis abridged their final plans on the errand and by 10.30p.m, they left the hotel bar room and were ahead of schedule by nearly an hour.

After registering in their hearts that the day had been well spent, Steve and Sheila left and drove in the heavy land rover to the country side where a decent residential house awaited to receive them, this was an area often referred to as The Black Hawk by the members of The Caliphs who knew it as "Masada Enclave" too, at the gate was a mean looking guy only called Fred. He looked into the car un amused, he unleashed the chains promptly and the two sides of the metallic gate fell ajar and the Landover rolled to the large parking place. The occupants of the car emerged from their seats and walked leisurely to the balcony of the thirteen-roomed mansion.

Inside the living room, there were three sets of sofa and at the far corner, a big Oak table stood and on top of it was a 32-inch Flat screen TV linked to a Digital satellite Dish. They made no move to settle in the living room and straight they marched had in hand to the staircase that led to the master rooms above. Soon they were nude and massaging each other in the twin bed. None of them was either aware that within a short moment that would be their final kiss or if ever they made a do, they would not be through up to the end. After much foreplay, they crowned the night with a round and drifted into deep sleep.

As Emmy and Davis neared the drive to the mansion, the security light at the gate brightened. All they could think of was to negotiate a rapid U-turn and had fast away. They had realized the dangers behind their moves. This mansion had only four people living in the fence.

Steve and his girl-the housekeeper and the man at the gate, occasionally could they allow two or more people into this fencing. There was an installed alarm protection system with a signal device fitted all round in the rooms and are some fifteen meters away from the gates. Should the switch be on, any intruder who reaches this buffer zone would be noticed in the house computer screens?

At this moment, Davis and Emmy abandoned the hunt and drove away like real rascals to the secret garage and disfigure that car a bit and do away with the false number plate. After 3.00 am, they had finished all that was necessary for his cover up. This relieved Emmy to put a call to Griffs and the latter informed Nick. "I'll step in." Nick said.

"It will be taken with much care". Griffs affirmed.

In the morning, Nick left his apartment and told Roselyn not to allow anybody beyond the gates and never to stay out till late hours. He was off to Cape Town in a fourteen-seater plane. On touch down, he telephoned Linda and told her that he would ring her after five hours. This in their secret code meant that should such a call flop, there was danger and the other could follow up.

He was off on his was and never even met Emmy nor could he tell Griffs that he was on the work. He went to the VR10 lane and in a booth; he rang the number Linda and told him some good period back. The phone was picked without delay. Sheila was on the other side and later Nick noticed this. "Hello, can I help you".

"Possibly... I would like to speak to your man".

"He is out to town". Sheila had snipped.

"It's urgent. Is he coming back soon"?

"I can't guess- May be after two hours" "Okay, I'll call later-'Bye"

Nick said and smiled to him on realizing that Sheila was a double-edged knife. Back in his car, he drove leisurely to Pearl and in a small Restaurant; he had an early lunch and continued his trip to Johannesburg. He arrived by the evening and spent the night in a nightclub dancing himself silly. This was the only occasion he had mixed freely with people in a social gathering since long. He retired at around two hours after midnight and went to sing for a room in a local lodging firm and spent the night in a fully relaxing sleep.

At dawn, he was shaken awake by a gloomy nightmare that Sheila was raising a gun at him. He came out of bed and sat thinking. Head rest in his palm so that he spent the wee hours trying to figure out what was happening.

Early in the morning after sipping an orange juice to sooth his dry throat and calming his nausea by having some light oil breakfast, he was on his way to Bloemfontein where he arrived by midday. He rushed with his lunch and headed fast to Welkom. He spent hours here sipping some gin and this set him in a better mental formulary.

At 4:25 p.m., he dialed again; it was Steve who spoke into the mouthpiece.

"Who are you and what do you want".

"Steve, It's me Warren. Important issues at hand, can we meet at Rosslee on the coast his afternoon"?

"I'll consider that but why can't we…"

"Then the noose will be no our necks"! Nick snapped and speeds up Steven's emotions.

"I'll be there by 5:00 p.m. on the do- make it a point".

"That's fine – 'Bye". Jackie replaced the receiver and hurried to the small airstrip to catch a piper plane to the Eastern Coasts of South Africa. He was in the hotel lounge by 3:20 p.m. and sipped a cold Heineken and relaxed by the pool side to enjoy and optical consumption of the clad bodies that roamed about on the tiled pool sides or those on the easy beach chairs.

He ordered a bottle of gin to be taken to his favorite escape parlor opposite the patio. As he gulped the first glass, Steve arrived and was shoved to the Patio side by the charming maiden at the Hotel.

If God offers luck and chances to some people, Nick should be counted among those. Steve couldn't show any suspicion for who he was. Hired on the job by late Alison Cook and he had never attended any of the closed sessions of the Black mind organization except that the person of T.R. Roberts nor his names.

Nick's dyed hair; his overcoat gave him a near perfection of Warren but not his voice. It was a matter of sheer credibility that Linda knew so well the operations of The Black Hawk, The Top Ten organizations and The Garments organization all associated with the Griffs group.

It was when Griffs had phoned him of Nicks' errand that Linda challenged, Emmy be informed about it and this so far had put Nick to a better footing thus how he was able to call Steve by name and also readily identify him from a group of men."

'Well done Stevenson, I like your time spirit"! "Thanks – Have you been here long"? Waving a hand to a seat across the table, Nick said, "Not long, I'm…….." He stopped short and asked "…something to drink".

"Thank you …some dry gin."

The waitress arrived immediately.

"Some dry gin for my visitor please". The blonde girl vanished and reappeared with the stuff and two were left alone to their glasses.

Minutes went by unnoticed, but each person was left to his private and dreadful dreams. However, sooner, it was Nick who broke the silence.

"Members, it has been a period of many surprises and disappointment but I would rather regard it as a package of shock and a scandal of mistrust!"

"That best describes it "! Griffs supplied while accustoming his grip on the slender curves of the small chalice glass.

"We have lost four key agents; the cover that we laid seems to be mere hazy gauze easily penetrated by the enemy eyes. They can now see us tens of kilometers away and our true identities are nearly blown".

Griff shook his head in agreement and relaxed to the chair to wait whatever orgies would unfold on him and all his lot.

"I personally feel that we stop using cellphones, as these are being bugged. No cellphones in whatever way but resort to public pay booths. We shall use our code name "Party Ten" and any mention of Scarce resource means take off immediately." Griff said.

"That's ideal and one disturbing bit is about our captive Joana and I'm having bad dreams that she may drop loose if we keep our systems relaxed", Nick challenged.

"Right now, she's in a secret room somewhere, under pricking eyes of my body guard Japheth and I don't think she will sneak out without a hole in her skull.

All that I made sure should run as arranged and should any breakthrough happen, we shall blow the house. I have an underground tunnel that will make our escape easy before sirens come into hearing."

"Well done Griff. You have done a lot. Thank you for all that job. Tomorrow expect a cheque for the extra deal. I will be seeing you soon. Boy! Nick snarled between clenched teeth. As their bottles stood empty the waiter arrived and picked the debris while tossing a bill/receipt to Jackie who paid immediately and the two heavy men rose to their feet and shared a firm and shake and vanished in either direction. That was step one in Nick's endeavors in the Joana files!

Linda was up in the fifth floor of Reste Corner Hotel, taking some milk to smoothen her ulcerating internals. She was in her favorite dressing, a faded Jean skirts and heavy jungle boots. A Glock 9 hung in the inner breast pockets of her jacket a fully drawn syringe tucked there as well. The time was 9.30 p.m and customers began filling the ballroom officials and the cream of the society there to drive away the tiredness of the day. Many were accompanies by their wives and even children. Life at that moment seemed as smooth as the shell of an egg.

Steve and Sheila were in the fifth row and helping themselves to a light beer. It was when the indoor music beaconed the song, "It's not forever"! That the audience joined in a harmonious clapper of hands and slow rhythmic shouts matching next to the musical jargon of the bikini clad performers on stage. The show of their legs by the girls was something Steve never wanted his eyes to miss a glimpse and at some moments the coloured knickers of the girls showed openly to the applause of the audience.

"Help God, they have put on Scottie miniskirts to kill our hearts and to light our hidden candles! Steve mumbled to his girls.

"That's the trick. Next time, there will be more ticket sales and that's what counts most but not the dignity lot on the stage". Sheila informed, "one minute, I feel I'll swell like the Mount of Olives!" Steve hissed into her ears.

"It's me who feels swollen and wet!"

"I can't imagine how"! Steve challenged.

"Your hand is touching me rather like me rather like sparking pug"! Sheila announced. Then here Steve realized that his left hand was dug into the waist zipping of her thin silken skirts and his fingers were massaging the crisp pubic hair around there. Immediately, he knew any step further, he would suffocate her and he withdrew his hand.

"Take me home, take me home". Sheila whispered into his ears.
"That is the next best thing I'm going to do"!
He affirmed and picking her hand, he led her through the aisle to the exit.

At last they were on the well paved compound with beautiful floral pots and well maintained garden feeling the cool breeze of African air and enjoying the Multi-million stars in the clear- blue African sky. "Chikera!" He whispered to her. They were in upholstered seats of the land rover. He turned the keys to ignition and the heavy engine roared into life. Engaging the reverse gear, he slump the car with a near squeak and shoved it ahead with a normal formal gear and they were heading home.

Linda has used the leather belts of an electrical engineer to fasten herself stiff onto the attachment of the fuel tank and the chassis. As the Rover hovered along the uneven roads, Linda only prayed to her few Gods tat the strap should never betray her. The Crisp sides of the belt drove into her groin and her back so mercilessly that she almost counted herself half dead as the motor-vehicle slowed down and some heavy chains rumbled and the gates were flung open, the spouse drove in and parked the Rover near and hawthorn flower and they disembarked as usual and walked side by side to the big door and that was a welcome home from a good evening they thought as the door was Slummed shut behind them.

Some three hours later, in the wee hours of the night, Linda had recovered fully from the pressure and cuts of the belts, as she lay on the cool and rough concrete in the parking yard. The night was cold and quiet except for noises of distant passing cars. The gatekeeper had retired to his small sentry box and the habitual up and temporary bed he set out of a duty coat and pieces of an old paper box, he was sound asleep.

Linda picked a tin of beef from her pocket and sprayed on it swallowed the piece and went into hiding without any smack of noise. This gave Linda the apparent time to tip toe to the man resting in the box and spray the same chemical to give the guard an added dizziness for sleep. She cut loose the electric cable that passed across the wall of the guard's room. With her pliers, she went further to disconnect the rear side cables from near the hind quarters and at last, she was satisfied with the success of her endeavours as she know the security plans to be. So far the alarm system was disorganised and what hell remained for her was the inter house movements.

Reaching the lavatory window, she picked her knife and peeled slowly the paned gluing and after a thirty minutes' struggle, the glass was in her hand and slowly, she placed it on the lawn. With her gloved hands, she slowly pushed the window ajar.

With a sluggish heave, she was in the tiled bathroom. By the great puzzle of chance, the door was left unlocked and the key hung like a leaf in its hole. Linda picked some shoe pads from her pocket and fastened them onto the sole of the boots to offer a cushion to avoid any clapper of her footsteps.

The pistol in her hands and walking along the wall side, she reached the stare case in the living groom that led to the rooms above. Stepping on the glossy carpet, with what tactical target of an assassin, Linda was able to realize a false floor beneath, bending low, she felt the carpet with her gloved fingers and felt a tiny depression of a line there. With a dazzling accuracy she picked the container of the liquid sleep drug and pacing the staircase, she squatted down to earth and administered good sprays under the doors of each room she bumped into. Now assured that her victims were attended to, she rejoined her task in the living room. With the sleek knife, she cut a meter-squared material from the carpet and with the help of the pencil torch; she gaped at the wooden cover on the hove. Pulling with that patience of a nun, she got the shock of her life when she got sight of the complex machine hidden there. Adjusting the flashlight, She read the instructions printed on it. Immediately, she clapped the switching knob to off and pulled the gadget out of its sinkage. Beneath, was a green army knapsack, drawing the zip down; she unraveled the contents on the carpet.

There was a 30 cm by 20cm booklet, measuring about 2 inches thick. She dashed this in her false pocket of the jacket. Again she found the 48 special and ten rounds of ammunition encased in the original factory package. Some used army jacket and trousers were there and the last thing she snatched was a passport for who ever!

She went back to the staircase and in front of the first door; she pulled a plastic syringe and drove in the keyhole some milliliters of nitric acid, the door opened inwardly. With her torch (flashlights), she found nothing of her taste apart from a study room; she knew searching the drawers would not bring her much harvest compared to the time factor.

She repeated this action in the second room and gosh, there was a women sleeping in a twin bed, with a multifold thought over a micro second, she guessed this to be Sheila. Quickly she drew her syringe of Pentothal v.6 and dug the needled thorough the coverlet and bed sheets, he piston of the gadget slopped. She breathed promptly to herself and left the room in a hurry. No sign of Steve!

In the third room, still no sign of Steve or Joanna, Linda knew then. She assumed that there must be a hidden room where Joanna must have been locked and Steve keeping guard. In a crazy speed to race fast away, she heaved herself through the window and not the lawn.

At the gate, there was still no sign of alarm, she decided to climb over the resting box and vaulted herself outside the fencing of doom! Running most of the way, she tumbled many times and at odd movements she hit her feet and felt the pun till after a long duration of merciless trespass and escape, she reached the elbow road, and Emmy showed up with only parking lights on and seated at the rear seat with an ooze gun was Nick, Linda dashed at the passenger seat and only managed to say: "Let's get lost the world is burning under my feet"!

By early morning at about 7.25 am, the three had reached Davis garage and all the weapons that they carried were sealed in an old drum and the false bottom welded. The drum was stocked among several other old drums in the scrap section.

After taking a light breakfast of soufflé and some bacon accompanied with strong coffee, the three left Davis smiling to himself with a heavy pocket of some Rand 500 and a promise for more contract and they boarded a sixteen seater plane and off to Lobatse.

Chapter 9

⌒*ℳ*⌒

THE FAILED PROMISE

Two months passed since Nick rejoined Roselyn in his small apartment in Lobatse, but he was not a happy man in the hollow of his heart. The fact that he never handled that Joanna issue himself and how Griffs managed to scoop Linda and match things up left a chronic scar in Nicks' heart. The thousands of Rand he had budgeted never came to him, but he found an easy way to Linda's private bag. Coupled with those unsuccessful rescue attempts by Linda and the most burning spot was the half-sketchy message Linda delivered to him. As Nick worked diligently to retrieve some important news about her personality, the Black Mind organization slapped him with an identification number to untie the guardian with his bank account, simmering to the bottom of the graph, a semi-permanent state of insomnia gripped him.

He was seated in his living room; his thought wavered like the cloud of smoke that emanated from his cigar. Why at all is he subject to the deceit and acts of "Jezebel," he termed Linda to be,

"A perfect Buccaneer"! He gasped aloud, and Roselyn appeared with a cup of Tea with Cocoa powder added to it. "Nod, bring me, Sherry"! He said.

"Your health seems to be deserting you of late, do please take tea and some sandwich," She reassured.

"Treat yourself to that or bring me nothing"! This last statement spun Roselyn around, and she ended up in the Kitchen with the contents on that tray finding their way to the sink. Her large white eyes were wet with tears. She arrived later and placed a bottle of sherry on the table with its accompanying glass. Sooner, Jackie was draining its.

As the boredom clenched his nerves, he began recollecting in his brain how he had met Roselyn in the first place!

Roselyn Sadie was traveling home on a public bus. She had just left her college on the outskirts of Kimberley. It was a memorable trip because Roselyn had awaited her transport for quite a time from her parents, who were on a farm in the far north; due to financial problems. Roselyn could spend most of her holidays working in the home of reasonably wealthy class members of Kimberly. Her talented work had initially been in Babysitter, which eventually turned into a baby maiden, but what she did most during her higher school life was housekeeping.

It had been her only source of income while at school.

Roselyn sat on the bus, but in her mind, she never dwelt much on her problems but rather her long-time yet worshipped village life. She had programmed that, if possible, she would drop by at her brother's house in Mafeking and possibly, takes a drive in his bonny swimming pool before reaching her parents and many friends back home.

Only on the eve of that trip did Roselyn receive a little sum from a sympathetic friend, Barbra, and she topped on her little savings from her work. As the bus drew nearer to the outskirts of Jo' burg, Roselyn began peeping through the window at the endless park of streaming pedestrians, the tree-lined streets, and the flowers that grew there to the fascination of approaching viewers.

The city traffic lights turned amber while driving as he negotiated the corners and headed to 6th street. As the bus stopped in front of the small restaurant Charanyama, her co-passengers bought some packed beef and bacon, but as to her diseased pockets, she just rested her back on the headrest support and pretended to dose. Her brain was thinking a hundred miles away about the galvanizing stories of her family life. Moreover, the confusion made Roselyn feel dizzy as the bus soon set off for the tour of Petersburg. Roselyn picked her photo album from her partly torn handbag and ran through the images of her schoolmates and friends up in the north and now as her eyes landed on the full-color print image of her boyfriend;- Paul, glancing with an acidic look. Now it melted into the sparking watery eyes of a kid. She had no college mates on the bus to chat with, let alone a few fellow students if ever they were there. Worrying about her and the life ahead, she fell fast asleep, and her album rested on her lap.

In a small suburb, before reaching yet another affluent town of Petersburg, the bus stopped in front of a Restaurant, and people began filing out for meals; the time was 6:45 pm like in college, but Roselyn slept longer.

Nick, seated in the backseat, rose and picked his empty thermos from a bag when the third last person stepped out. She was a stout lady in her late forties. Passing with the flask to the door, Jackie reached Roselyn's seat and called out. "You do travel on an empty torso, hey?" there was no answer.

After patting her lightly on the shoulders, Roselyn was left electrified and awoke from her dizziness jubilantly and stared into the small white pair of eyes looking down at her. The question had been more of a Command, she thought. Roselyn had wanted to say something, but her internal clock sounded, "Time to feel the void" What if I say, mind your own business? She thought fast. Jackie bent to pick her album from the floor and gave it to her. 'Thank you, "she forced with a little smile, fearing this man. She hesitated further a little, but as Jackie made up his mind to go realizing her childish behavior, Roselyn replied, "But I mean, I don't have bucks." The words dry, and her throat rough. She felt the pang, but her eyes dilated as Nick stopped, peeled an R100 note, and tossed it to her without saying any word. She clasped the note to her palm and whispered in a throaty voice, "Thanks very much, Mr...."

Her lips slanted for failing to pronounce his unknown name; Nick walked out, picking his flask from the seat he had laid it on. Rosalyn hastily tossed her album into her bag and rushed to take a meal. She remembered having last tested one for the day at 6.30 am in the college, which was their traditional porridge.

She was in the hotel. Nearly all the tables are not accessible except for a few in the far corner. As she paced her way through to the well-lit interior of the room, he almost bumped into Nick, who said, "This way, I have ordered a meal for two"!! She hated being alone with him, but what was the harm anyway? As she thought, she realized the man had turned to go to a table in the far corner facing the patio. The feelings left her with only one civilized option to follow the man. As they sat to meet each other from across the round table, the waiter arrived with a meal of chicken, chips, and nice stew to accompany it. There was a stew of Irish in separate bowls as preliminary. As she sat there nursing her appetite with the delicious meal, the only other inclusion on the table stalled her brain, and her body cockpit failed for the moment. There were petals of roses on the tray.

Nick ate with his fancied chicken tikka and left her enjoying a plate of rice and egg curry. He was paying the bill and walked out carrying his thermos filled.

As she raised her neck to gaze over the rest of the room occupants, she almost got no glimpse of the waiter who placed a jug of orange juice on the table. There was no flicker of idea in Roselyn's mind to think about asking any detailed questions, for she already knew that all were from the chaperon hands of this stranger.

A moment later, on the bus, she felt moved into loving this man who cared significant about her but said nothing to clear her doubts. "A good Samaritan...." She thought. She had expected a formal introduction, and that seemed next to impossibility.

The next stop was at Petersburg by 9:20 pm, and nearly all left to book rooms for the night, but Roselyn lagged behind any casual standards that Nick Morgan could find a room with a twin bed. Turning to pace the staircase from the main reception, he faced the idle woman again. He tossed her those keys without saying words, but she spoke to the fat Tswana lady at the chairs behind the ample wooden counter."

"The last room has been booked off"! The waitress replied. She strolled behind him to the room, and he hurled his bag and briefcase, and he was out of the room.

Roselyn had only to drop her bag and sit on the velvet chair by the bedside. Many people went to the recreation center, and others went for late evening shopping in the numerous groceries and supermarkets. She, on her part, was licking her bruises in that armchair. When Nick knocked at the door of room 202, it almost jerked Roselyn from her hazy mental formula. She hesitated a little but damned herself for what shit she was doing. After all, it was his room, and what right had she to shut him out? Roselyn gathered all her effort to turn the keys, and as the lock gave the clicking sound, Nick had shoved it wide open and was already involved. Roselyn missed the push-off by his masculine body by a mere distance of hair touch.

At the same time, she locked the door again without a fitting composure of her mood.

Jackie was seated on the chair next to the bed, peeled off his dirty green jacket, and rested it on the back of the chair.

His chest muscles heaved in the light blue T-shirt, making Roselyn sick with curiosity and desire to know him a bit more.

"I'm very sorry; we are sharing the room. There was nothing else I could do" Nick stopped tense and sounded casual. Roselyn failed to talk. She began paraphrasing her vulnerability in the hands of this stranger.

"Maybe you tell me who you are and what job you did before. I am Roselyn Sadie, a student from an accounting college, Kimberley." She said.

"Thanks for your introduction, but I deem it unnecessary, Miss. Sadie."

"That's not logical, at least; I can't."

"If you can't serve sleeping here well..." He jerked his head to one side, almost implying, 'I don't care, it's up to'! Now, where could she go? To the bus and curl herself in the back seat? No. The possible since he stood in her life as one who cares. The time is 11:50 pm; what would she do in the remaining hours of the night?

Who knows what would happen. After much serious thought, Sadie spoke again,

"Maybe you have the bed, and I make one for myself on the floor with a sheet."

"You have the bed and I and take the chair," Nick continued.

"No. The bed is yours". Roselyn felt a temptation build in her mind, and she reassembled her defense weapons to tackle Nick.

"I didn't intend to shut you up with me but take that we are victims of circumstances. I need to sleep now" he stood up and took off his traveling shirt. His chest muscles reveal some hidden perfection in his build-up.

The curled hair on his abdomen was like grass in a well-maintained botanical garden. Nick fidgeted, buckling his belt, and a pair of denim descended to his heels and stepped out of the mass. In his tight sports undies, he strode to the bed, picked the blanket and a sheet, and handed them to Roselyn, saying, "I don't run on gals without preliminaries. `Save yourself when she set herself a bed on the far corner. He had already slipped into bed and snored heavily.

Roselyn lay packed in her dressing and covered in the light silken sheet.

Thoughts flooded her brain. There was no comfort in bringing the needed sleep. After tiring herself till 2.30 am, worrying all the time, she began retracing all the stranger said. The man seemed harmless. He lay on the edge of the bed, leaving most of it vacant as though he was used to sharing beds. Now, who was there to fill the void?

It couldn't be Sadie; she could snuffle beside him and let things happen because all her efforts had deserted her.

Roselyn got up and picked up the sheets from the floor. She undressed nude waist up and a gossamer dress and knickers below. Stealthy, she passed over him and lay in the void towards the wall; just as she was drawing up her free sheet to cover herself, the man spoke, and his voice was like thunder in her being, "Back home from self-exile "!

She charged, "So you have been watching me undress"? She gasped in shock and felt the pains of shame cascade through her body as she pronounced her nudity.

"I've seen shapes, colors, and sizes; I'm not a proclaimed Juno award hero, and I'm not here for talks- good morning." He rolled to one side of the bed, and he was sound asleep after a while. Subconsciously, Roselyn was curled in the hollow of his back and felt his warmth suffuse her body into a tense sleep, and she lay facing his behind. Chagrined, Roselyn relaxed in bed. She thought about why and how she was vulnerable and what has he done to her. What has what has said? Why does she feel so-so weak and mentally in a revolution? Why? Why does she feel the urge to talk to him, and why is she haste to know him better and touch him a bit if that way? To fulfill her feelings that seemed to reach a crisscross state of shape?

She slept when her mind had covered a thousand more horizons, all of which were registered. The subconscious mind never rested. It was interpreting her emotion into play:

Nick was on her chest. The two of them inflated with breath as though they were gas cylinders. He was kissing her throat, and his hands were massaging her neck, bringing them the feeling of a sensitized harmony. He was groaning and whispering lovely voices into her ears' smooth, soft skin. She, on her part, was hissing smooth codes of affection to him. She laid her hand on his chest, enjoying the touch of the brittle hair there. Then she laid the other hand on his back, stroking the deep valley along his spine. Sooner, his hands moved to the warmth of her inner thighs, touching quickly like a thousand small pins pricking her heart.

Then, he felt her knickers, which flew tenderly down her heels and off. She opened up to the central cavity of her being- welcoming his entrance.

"Maybe we postpone this? ` He was muttering.

"No, No...You can't. I'll never." Her voice had reached utter frustration that it woke him from his sleep. He came up in a thrust and switched on the small reading lamp by the bedside. Sitting upright, he shook her violently that she was back to her senses and reality with one touch, her eye flimsy with tears of ecstasy aroused by her dream. He still held her shoulders.

"What's wrong"?

"Nothing..." As his grip on her hardened, she continued saying, "just nothing." She was lying because a shiver ran through her body as she felt his strong arms on her.

"Are you sure you are alright"?

"I'm fine Sorry; I woke you"? She had wanted to ask, 'What did I do'? But he had read her mind already.

"You were crying, shouting, and kicking." Just as he pronounced this last word, she gazed at her half-covered body, and her lips parted in shock. The gossamer under clothing was wrapped around her hip, exposing a good portion of her thighs; worse, her legs were apart! His gaze followed hers, but before she could admit embarrassment, he drew the coverlet over her.

When she forced dry lips, "Thanks, "his eye was on her lips." His sleep turned small light brown eyes wandered to the over-taxed veins around her neck and then down to her breast. He unleashed his grip on her, descended on his back, and opined cool, "I hope you'll have a dreamless sleep-Miss, Sadie," she was. Numb – for his depicting capability. She wanted to deny it, but her lips opened only to release a gasp. He was in bed, but this time was not sleeping- she thought sadly. He glanced at his Chrono and switched off the light".

Roselyn slept till 7.30. It was not a topic in her daily life. At least in school, she had grown used to waking up before 6.00 am. Worse still, Jackie ushered her forward for the day when she felt his touch on her chick.

"You sleep like a lamb, Miss. Sadie." He enabled her to eat breakfast and warned, "we will be here for twenty minutes before our departure." Though Sadie predicated some hidden thoughts in the smugness on his face, he sounded like an old friend. He did not attempt to leave the room, though.

"Thanks for the bother." She made as if coming out of bed, but her consciousness forbade the cause. How can I get to dress in his gaze?

Why do I feel jelly-like in his presence? Then why this added heartbeat and nausea?

"About last night, I apologize "! He eased himself, having read her mind.

"You are not to blame."

"I think I hold half that or more. Again observe time" Nick padded to the door and was out before she formed a comment. The patter of his footsteps echoed in her head long enough as she hurried in her dress and made for the bath.

Sadie took a cold shower in the lady's room, and the water spray through soothing had tormented her ego to an uncompromising degree. When finished, she finally dried herself from the spare towel before rushing to glance at her reflection in the mirrors. All she saw was a lady older than herself with lines of dizziness across her face. Her eyes were two empty holes of pity to her disgracing, fumbled curly hair. She dropped the towel on the rail where Nick used the other one. She bent to smell it and got the scent of his aura, and all her emotions went into crisis. "Stupid," she ordered herself.

She added a bit of makeup and lipstick lightly once she was in the bedroom.

In her beg, there were few beautiful dresses she could pick to defend her feelings; after a rapid thought in only some thirty seconds, she dressed in a black dress with yellow flowers at the breast. Added to her dressing was a necklace with a silvery jade on which had a printed letter "H," which was her 22nd birthday gift from her aunt Hellene. She was startled by the knock on the door. All along. She didn't even hear the approaching footsteps. Why has he knocked if he had stubbornly cheated my privacy last night? Is he showing gentleman-ship now after a disarray minutes ago? Maybe he knows that I'm dressing. "Come in," she gasped in a voice she regretted later.

It was the bed-dresser.

"Hello. Good morning, Miss. Sadat".

"Good Morning." Sadie managed to force a smile, and her heart recoiled from the mispronunciation of her name. "It's Sadie, but call me Roselyn. Can I help?

"It's alright. Just to dress up the beds. Hope you had a nice comfortable rest."

"Just do your job, okay"? She retorted. How can I correct this woman and give her my other name? How has she learned that I'm still single to attach a 'Miss' so carelessly like that? The stranger again! Why when is this woman talking to me as if I was part of her acquaintance?

"Crazy"! Roselyn said aloud just as the woman spread new sheets on Nicks' bed and picked the used ones along.

"Maybe I've troubled you"?

"No. I was just thinking of the boring travel ahead"! She opined levelly. The room attendant excused her later, clutched the used sheets under her armpits, and yanked the door shut behind her. Roselyn was to her conflicting emotions again. If this man doesn't tell me his name or more, I'll never take a sip of his coffee. I can't tolerate serving doubt without questions. Anyway, I'm no lean meat for him, and how can I be? How I've my lovely child to nurse not the attention of thirty-two teeth self-centered a stubborn bastard. Why should I care to be polite to him when he lacks interest? 'Let him go.'

Roselyn assured herself. After all, she is a survivor in biological terms with a handsome kid of her own. It's not her fault, the corners of her brain challenged- but hers and of a confectionery work. The memory painted a dull disappointing image in her mind. She was in her end-of-year exams. She went with him for an evening the day before she would be back at her college. What was a casual outing went further than that? He urged her in his borrowed car and drove her to a small pub and later to his apartment. Waving aside all her protests later in his room, he pestered her to undress for him. "No. Please not now. It's the red channel. I promise to make her breast."

"If you love me, then don't do it, darling. Are you listening to me? She pressed her defense. He groaned deep inside and murmured something she did not hear, and her body turned weak. She loved him just that much, but the thought of doing the scene obstructed her wisdom; at last, he won.

Back in college, she missed one significant body function the following month. The second month, she drew all her body flags at half-mast. She was doomed. During one conference, the principal added one particular address to the girls after his speech. "My dear female students, this evening we shall have a visit by a Doctor; it's part of our routine inspection, but I'm sorry, this had to be rushed ahead by weeks. Your usual co-operation is needed. Failure is the worst sin-Remember", He said. His voice was engraved in her mind in block notes of lines and echoed with harshness. Then, the college authority netted three girls, and she was one of them who got sacked from school with a small letter to their parents.

"… Your Daughter ceases to be our student following the reports of our doctor. She had been found pregnant for her since our facilities do not stretch for such cases. You might be disappointed just as we were shocked with the same message. Let's give a face to facts".

Back home, when she presented the letter to her mother, she glared and turned fury!

"You are not done with your responsibilities" That was all she said. Roslyn's mother, who had been her shield and source of inspiration, always lent a shoulder to cry on, but on this incidence, she broke out into shatters of dismay. The worst to face rebuke was her Dad. Neither her brother nor sister offered support, not even comfort. She could be devastated by the wrong attitude of family members. When she came out of her handrail, she swore never to allow any opposite sex to look down on her rails of life-Never again! She had sworn. Tears of self-pity rolled over her cheeks, and a heavy masculine hand wiped them away.

"Don't think about it; if it inconveniences you, can you stop crying then, baby."

His hand moved to her shoulders and turned her to face him. She was numb to resist his touch. A heavy icy lump filled her throat.

"Have I done you a curse, Sadie? Maybe. "She had come to the realm of reality when his lips touched hers lightly. She had not known when Jackie entered the room nor why he dried her cheeks of childish tears. Now he released his grip on her and said coolly, "Now coffee will do you good…" she stepped backward in anger for having relaxed and submitted in his hands and yet not asking her throbbing questions. "I don't want your coffee. Just let me out of here2. She rushed to the bedside to pick up her traveling bag and hurried to the door, almost stepping into the wide corridor and the outside world.

Nick's hand fell on her shoulder again, and he spun her round to face him by a race of a mere blinking of the eye. Her eyes met his. Two small bifocals, reddish brown, returned her gaze. Her face dropped, and the large shady eyes peered at his flat stomach, then down past his belt and back to his face. No mistake, he was angry.

"Stop playing possum with me; why were you crying? Why did you kiss me? She asked. "Because you despised me and wanted me altogether."

"Liar, Liar! You're not a topic in my life. I don't know why you should continue looking at me like that"!

"Our breakfast is running cold," he informed. When he drew Roslyn towards an armchair, Roselyn said nothing and pushed her onto it. He picked up his cup and emptied it while almost finishing the second sandwich in his hand. She had done nothing. "Stop this childish drama," He snarled, "I thought you were a woman, and such people usually."

"That'll lead you nowhere" The words came out without thought, and she regretted them later.

"Poor little girl, I don't encourage you to have second impressions about me."

"Then tell me who you are," she pressed further.

"I'm not a topic in your life- Remember you said," He waited for a deliberate pause. Then continued, "What did the bed dresser do"?

"Nothing, I was just thinking about this odd journey" she was taking her coffee now. After all, oh, did Nick say 'poor little girl? So he helped me because I was easy prey? It was over three years since she underwent the most depressing phase of her life; now, this must be another? He picked up his briefcase and bag and hung hers on his shoulder.

"The journeys on, Miss Sadie"! She rushed after him closing the door behind her.

She attempted to grab her bag from his hand in the long corridor but without success. Roselyn glimpsed a Toyota Celica sports at the hotel parking area with beaded upholstered seats, a polished wheel, and a comfortable suiting windscreen tinted light brown, just a convenient dashboard.

She whistled subconsciously.

"If you have trouble going by bus, then try the smaller friend" He hurled their luggage on the backseat and turned to open the passenger door for her, but the waitress arrived with the bag of packed lunch that Jackie had ordered earlier, and this was hurled onto the back seat as well. He yanked her to the center with a little force, and before she could utter protests and curses, he was behind the wheel, and the engine came to life.

"Where are we going"? She asked.

"Where your choice lies," He snarled. The car Swept from the Packard onto the smooth tarmac, and off they went.

Ahead, Nick saw an old avid well-attended street stall ripped bodily off the ground by a gust and hurled at a packed audience, watching the passersby from a shop veranda wrenching their vision of the holidaymakers. Nick is the perfect man who, as a Merlin, matched evenings to dusk, dusk to dawn, and mornings so that all through no hour goes for a cater. The perfect time killer and an emotional tableau! She thought.

"I want to be the center of events; from now on, don't ever leave me or behind any scene. You get that"? He read her mind quickly and readily supplied this commentary.

"I don't think you'll win"!

"I always win," he said.

'Not this time when I'm a party to the game".

"Just that, and I don't give up easily." This last pronouncement sank into the fabric of Roselyn's brain and her admission that she was a party to the game. So I'm trapped with myself as the bait?

Never happen-I can't happen again, not to me! She reassured herself for the thousandth time and pitied herself for failing most of the time. When she lived with her aunt Helen, she had taken her lessons. Keenly and every lecture party was still fresh in her mind in block iron letters: Men are the most dangerous human images. They always want to get what they can't have.

It's by the trickery of false faithfulness or force, so watch out. The results obtained from such a business are always the same. THEY WIN. Roselyn was assured. Her uncle also told her that men couldn't tell you their principles openly, but they lived a lifestyle you can understand after a long time. You discover if you are lucky. This sodden information about men had been passed from their legendary parents down to the present family members- with little alterations except more additions to give flavor and understanding. The changing pattern of life was more dynamic to perceive and capture.

Men, it was said, whatever dirty job comes their way, they do it for money, tell their wives nothing, and go where they think big money lies; that is the motto they follow.

Loose ladies ran errands for their fellow rich men who woe young girls and are the dons behind the brothel business. They, too, con people's wives and still call themselves respectable men! Sometimes they send a few bottles to their busy wives within an elbow's distance. The men supply information for sale and still maintain the habit of always waiting to sleep with the ladies in their houses. Then, they call on one hand and the customers at another; they pick off any quid intent for the service girl, and yet they laugh most when you are behind bars in a police cell. They say, "The whores are in their pit again"! And cheers of conquering follow.

On festive occasions, they book hotel rooms for people of dignity and help transport or escort cool girls to their rooms, and at odds, they want to sleep with these girls too! Our feelings aren't necessary for the business. Your cries, protests, hate, and even kill you at last – Whatever ways; they are the masters of the world. That's what's most important of all"! Roselyn closed her eyes as she clamored to be free of the grip of this male domination of the world.

"What's up"? She asked as the car drew up outside the gate of a beautiful house. They were in Messina.
"Just to inspect the house, I intend to buy. Do you mind joining me for the tour" it wasn't a question?

Zero! I can't it's not my house anyway" Anyway is a word of losers in a game, her aunt snipped into her filled-up ears.
"Make it yours by acting sensibly."
'If your house is a watch without the hour hand, so it can't fit you because of me, sorry, try another source.' She aggressively supplied her side of the coin.

"As if you can't suffice," He said, casting a side-glance at her, and she felt his eyes burn a hole in her skin.

"That and I'm not your compliment."

"Evil, whoever tells you that you are incomplete to suit me. Secondly, who tells you I'm in search of, Err..." he let the sentence hang deliberately long enough to stir reactions within her and let him dashed straight to the point. "...You are eaten up with jealousy"! It turns out that she was jealous. He was the perfect pilot with whom she could feel woman enough. Her feelings would go anywhere they pleased, yet the comfort wouldn't lack any delirious bit; all would match a perilous escape if only she could accept the reality. She could trap her rolling and sagging mood. She would forget the entire girlish gospel her elder sister had pumped into her and the nonsense dogma of older women to young girls. She would be her guest and manager of her feelings. She would be free.

He was already walking the curved steps into the living room. Inside, the well-furnished room. As Roselyn followed leisurely after him, she peed into the main bedroom and gasped on seeing the porcelain flower pot and the magnificent and reclusively large bed-the tufted carpet. Jackie emerged from the study room only to find Roselyn fascinated by this cozy room.

"...am..." The sentence dragged on her lips as an immediate word could not come out. "Let's have some lunch" this was to her relief as she later acknowledged that her body clock was running off. She ceased to this idea.

In the dining room, they shared that highly romantic garlic stew and hamburger with petals of roses flying heartily on the tray. They shared little talks and washed it down with some bit of wine, as was her favorite drink at that time.

"Welcome to my home." He announced proudly, sipping some wine.

"I would have said thanks if it was formal, but my entry was rather..." she challenged.

"You sound skeptical yet amusing." As Nick confidently entered his gust room and smiled, his curved lips with cheeks showed dimples. His drowsily dimmed, intense eyes caused her internals to warm up with some hidden desire so profound that when his hands crossed the table and caressed her fingers, she turned jelly-like and enjoyed that rotations touch. Their fingers entangled, and the warmth from his hairy hands was like doses of electrical massaging, which tilted her brain towards Nick.

"I must apologize for being rude at times, but it has not been part of my daily practice to draw into intimacies with the opposite sex," he said.

"That's one thing, but who you are bothering me, hell."

"You can call me Nick Morgan; I work for an audiovisual device company," He supplied to her.

"That qualifies you for top most mimicry- thanks for your introductions."

"And for your compliments," He teased. A half-moon smile had cornered Roslyn's face. Unconsciously she was a sibling that faded, which hurled in the cool of her neck. Jackie took this chance to look at her lips, her breasts, and his eyes descended till the tabletop restricted them in his explorations of her body. "I'm growing out of patience. Last time I saw you board the bus, second when you fell asleep in the seat, especially your closed eyes with those cloudy lashes, I was put off only when you turned timid".

"Any other woman would recoil under such circumstances."

"Not when I proved harmless."

"But your hidden identity made me…."

"Desire me, particularly to know me better." She smiled as she tapped her chin. Her hands did not deflect his hands; then, it urged him to move to her side and brush a kiss on her nose; she slowly bit her lips, and her mount opened to allow his tongue access to visit her mouth. He ran his tongue smoothly on her upper teeth. She felt gyrated.

"Nick, don't. You should not." She gasped, with her breathing dropping considerably.

"I don't mean to hurt you. It's this bemused look on your face, that hard-to-read complexion which sort of drives me crazy, and I find it hazily simmering when I touch you and best when I'm kissing you."

"I don't know how you are feeling right now but trust me, you are not so much yourself today" He rose from her side and picked her hand. She followed lazily behind him to a wide corridor till they emerged at the hindquarters.

"What's up?" she hissed. Just ahead was a large compound with the fence some 50 meters away. There was a small pineapple garden that punctuated the papaw trees.

On their side was a well-kept flower garden. In the middle of the compound was a swimming pool that had captivated Roslun's fascination. She clung to his chest.

"I must apologize on the second note. "This is my house and yours," she said. He deliberately broke the sentence that when he had finished, she was numb.

"I don't seem to be understanding." She managed at last just precisely what I've already said. He held her tenderly to his chest and made a deep kiss on her lips that when she dragged-rather carried her to the beach chair nearby; her defenses were all but broken. Massaging her things in minute strokes that seemed almost electric, he undid the zip of her dress and helped her out of it; she helped remove his shirt, and he motioned her to the buckle of his belt that concealed her womanhood.

He started a ravaging kiss from her inner things and navel, and when their lips glued, he was between her thighs; she was eager to take him when he withdrew from the kiss as though to say something good. "Maybe I should not do that."

"Ja…" she groaned and dug her fingers into his back that he only knew she was urging him to make the score. With trained care, he slipped in, bolting the two separate souls into what later became Mr. And Mrs. Rolovin, crowned with orgasms by both partners and a bottle of champagne.

That was how Roselyn entered Nick's bandwagon and persevered through the years of hardship, happiness, and most of all, the long-awaited joy she would derive: she carried Nick's baby. He had seriously discouraged that.

"Not now, honey, it will come by sometime only one baby...we shall have. All her efforts to conceive have broken down by this self-styled-mannered – Nick.

Chapter 10

THE QUIET INVESTIGATION

Now, as she sat in his living room, at last, he had reached an agreement between his reasons for first loving Roselyn and now dropping the affair in which she of late acquired a habit he neither appreciates nor feels he could tolerate in his life.

She had finished serving meals on the table, and he joined her to eat that stew lettuce sauce and some rice. They both sat at the table on the same side, and there was little they shared in talks except for Roselyn's forced holiday to Zimbabwe.

"After three months' stay, I'll have to come right back and take a course in computer science especially spread sheet using lotus 1-2-3".

"You have to remain there till you hear from me."

"What if you delay ringing to me"?

"You'll keep waiting."

"I'll...." She started, but her words faded as a drop of tears rolled down her cheeks." I never branded you to be such type of Sado-Maniac or what"!

"Call me anything, but I'm well balanced in my emotional orbit, and I've gone through that phase; you are in its part of being what the world has turned me upside down. Before you brace your anger too much, I 'would point that get going, there are a few corns you may pick by, as for me, the rate we among the jewel turned to ashes"! She looked and him, tense and agape. She dropped the spoon and fork and stood up to go and pack her safari bag. He made no move, nor did he say any word.

Roselyn emerged later with her belongings. In her eyes were anger, rage, and a dangerously unpredictable eyes of a psychopath. She sat on the high stool by the paper of a book he had been delving into a couple of days ago. He was delving so profoundly that he missed the first attempt to sight a colored feature in the dull yellowish pages of the old novel, "Not the last "! On the second trial, he caught sight of it, scooped that paper photo-type replica, and looked at the innocent young face that looked him back.

Roselyn portrayed herself in her twenty-second year wearing a silken blue dress with some embroidery of yellow patches; on her ear lobes were jaded rings. Her eyes whitened and somewhat brightened. Her African mane of hair just dropped about her nape, giving her an almost ice-syrup look.

He emerged in the sitting room, paced reluctantly to take his seat, and crossed his legs with ease once he was comfortable with those upholstered cushions.

"I think this is the beginning of the end of my insomnia," He said."

"The start of yet another-you could say..." she opined while composing herself.

"This thought has been bugging my head stiffly, and the question is how you allowed Linda to scope my secrets and my life...."

"Do understand me this time; she claimed that you were in a trap and those records were the price of negotiations for your life, and it was because I loved you that much and cared about your life, so I released them just for you. Jack."

"You sold me off, especially my identity."

"Not knowingly or intently, but it was a double coincidence of mischief, which I wasn't knowledgeable till later- Do you still call me bad"?

"Not exactly; I've no vocabulary for branding people."

"In your eyes, just behind it, I see resentment." Roselyn pressed further.

"I'm not into partnership with an unprecedented cohabitation infidelity."

"Your temper may govern you to say that, but to me, it was only a mishap."

"From then on, I knew things would never be any better," He leveled.

She had cooled from her flaring anger and was in a solemn mood to talk to him. On his face were dreamy lines around the eyes, and his lips slanted more to the left, and most of the time, he talked, looking at the space between his legs. The photograph kept hanging within his slender masculine fingers till he found a gas lighter from his pockets and lit the printed paper from the bottom. A flame so yellow cum bluish emanated from the substance till unconsciously he kept it too long in his hands that the heat touched on his skin, he dropped the sheet to the floor and sooner it was a black sport of ashes on that tiled floor.

"Yeah, that crowns it –" She hoaxed, tears rolling down her cheeks.

She stood up and started carrying her briefcase and handbag towards the door.

"My mind seems." She stopped at the door and looked him over her shoulders, but he said no more words and pinned there; she made no advance nor withdrew. It was like standing at the edge of a cliff- a state of indecision in her.

Nick rose heavily from his seat, then paced towards where the rest of her belongings lay, at the entrance to the study room. She made no effort to stop him but instead placed down her briefcase. He helped carry her luggage as she ferried the small handbag to the smallness of the Estate Wagon. He opened the passenger side of the doors and saw that Roselyn had some trouble with her departure. He never bothered but placed her luggage on the back seat and moved to her, picking her coast from her hand. He turned to his side, and as he closed the door, Roselyn snarled one thing, "Will you be lonely"? That's one thing, but I'll be busy with my job". He glanced at her as she sat in the hollow of the car seat and saw she was miserable, he held her cheek in his palm and kissed her passionately, and she wanted to cry.

She was feeling lonely herself and wished his strong hands could grip her waist like that and always. She shuddered and said, "May I ask, what's your last answer to the question"?

'I've not changed my mind".

'I repeat, what do you think about a marriage between the two of us"? Her eyes were flimsy with tears. The pain in her mind was that her parents would be shocked by her second failure with a man she would come out of the agonies of a personal curse she had accredited. Her hopes for finding a man in her life to have a happy marriage with two kids sprawling the rooms, veranda, and shouting on the compound while she is in the kitchen making a nice meal for her "dream family" was fading away. How posh it could be to feel the aura of Nick by her side in that queen bed and how cozy it could all sound to her kids giggling in the next room and the morning that would usher them to the next phase of life. The biting question was how her life could emerge fragmented by repeated failures in relationships with men. And her long-awaited wedding!

"I would say, rethink before your world crumbles before your face and you lick the shit of women the world has maintained, especially when your next target is Linda."

"Then you are out of my calendar"! Said he

"I credited you with a better answer than that." Her fingers landed on his chest and massaged the brittle hair there.

"I mean it, Roselyn. It wasn't meant for me that way, and if I forge one with you, you'll never be happy."

"Why"? Rang on her lip, "Because of your job"?

"That's the other side of the coin" She saw no pity in his eyes, looked down at her feet, and sobbed. He touched the keys on the keyhole, and the engine echoed to life. Roselyn was so depressed that she considered herself a shit of paper in the dustbin in his eyes. A squeezed orange of a woman! As others say, not suitable for his taste whatsoever.

He drove off to the airfield, and their trip was not engaging with talks. At the airport, Roselyn jerked the door open and came out. He helped pick up her luggage from the luggage compartment of the car.

"You do hate me"? She said weakly, avoiding his face.

"Have a good holiday, Baby" his memory switched on the bad memories that the female generation seemed to leave on his and how Roselyn had hit the upper limit of infidelity. He stood by the side of the car as she projected her destiny ahead. Involuntarily she dropped in his mighty hands and kissed him lightly, and he released her quickly, saying,

"Of all ladies I know, please admit to yourself my mind still writes my name upside down, and I'm not so sure how long this will last"! He was already behind the wheel and sped away before she uttered a word.

Chapter 11

⌒∿⌒

THE CALIPHS AND THE ARABIAN PENINSULA LINK

Ramadan Sebi was a marine assistant plying the Somali coast of Kismayu to Yemen, taking camel meat and bringing electronics, perfumes, and running errands for some wealthy warlords on the mainland living in Mogadishu. These warlords had many vessels on the Indian Ocean. Some contraband items like ivory smuggled from the Northern Kenya parts of Turkana with main centers like Kamuka, Kapenguria, and Lokichoki, which found accessible markets in the Arabian Peninsula in Oman, Yemen, and parts of Jordan. Ramadan and the team would enjoy the Ocean rides for months, and life at sea looked more appealing, luxurious, and desirable. They met several smaller vessels with bigger ones and exchanged fresh fruits, whiskies, and beef, and sometimes they would drop some ladies back to the mainland after having some good fun in the waters. They would often sneak into some free zones and just camp to have fun, away from the pirates and snoopy eyes of the US marines, constantly patrolling the Eastern Coast for any suspicious movements of cargo and people. Some days later, a group of extremists went as far as the Indian Ports of Mumbai. They brought agricultural tools and fertilizers, which some dirty groups use for operating in cells for manufacturing rudimentary explosives; these guys were well read and did military training of IED-Improvised Explosive Devices from Tehran and Kabul. They are a hazardous team and classified as very deadly on the US watch list.

We experienced that life on the ocean was more blissful than on the mainland. There were many opportunities to meet people of profound backgrounds whose primary interest was delivering vast sums of money to the mainland and a few weaponry; this was more than what a young marine assistant would bargain for our delivery of goods. It made life easy and appealing that recruiting many young boys into this lifestyle was simple, but trust and honesty were the most complicated part of this trade. It depends on how good you are at keeping secrets, not how much you are willing to take. On odd occasions, some boys got their throats slit open by their bosses on suspicion or upon receiving conflicting stories about them. It was a game of money, right, but trust first.

Ramadan is trusted because he keeps close to the bosses; he knows who deals in what and learns their likes and dislikes, the foundation of this thriving illicit trade on the Indian Ocean. No one wanted to be called a pirate; this was very demeaning to them because they knew they had a right over the waters to do any business of their choice. Many of his colleagues got wealth and great exposure from this business; they learned of great places by plying on the waters. Having spent over four years traveling to cities like Oman, Mumbai, and Mombasa, he had got acclimatized with the Eastern Coastal areas. He was fluent in Kiswahili, Arabic, Amharic, and English. He was capable of delivering goods worth 10,000$ and above, which earned him loyalty.

Ramadan was fairly educated among his peers because he was capable of servicing the engines of these boats and doing maintenance.

One fateful day, they had in their company some Ethiopian Belles with whom they were merry-making. The party started right from the coast when they set sail. Clara and Carol were the intelligent girls on the boat, but the most striking figure and personality were that of Morita; she was so curvy and well built. She stood tall, muscular with athletic strides. She would cause a commotion as she walked aboard the Ship floor. The captain was so glued to her that no one was allowed into his cabin without authority. The rest of the sailors enjoyed the cool brisk air with lots of mutton and grilled camel meat. They washed it down with Iranian coffee and green beer. The group had been roving on the water for days as they killed their lust for a specific location, swayed further east into the ocean, and the US naval ship guard managed to capture the group. The US naval guards kept them captive on the waters for four months; they subjected the prisoners to torture, denied them good sleep, and starved them for several weeks as their captors enjoyed mutton and whisky. They were often treated to some rationed meals as they awaited their release. Ramadan had lost all contacts, and they snatched his savings. He was more deeply affected than other crew members since this was his first time being captured by high-class officers, apart from little encounters with the local Pirates. It was often a matter of cash changing hands and losing a few expensive Jeans and Jackets, but life was much more accessible. The increased US presence in the Indian Ocean has affected lots of trade among the African and Arabian Countries for the past decade. Arabs countries are rapidly growing their presence in the African continent through scholarships to Universities. Some of these attractive universities are; Jeddah, Tehran, and Kuwait universities for African students. These universities have vested interests in African students studying; Islamic laws, Islamic Banking, Agriculture, and Information Technology, but they keep them far from studying courses in Petroleum and Surveys, which the Arabs and Asians restricted to their kids back home.

The motive for taking many African students for these courses was through the Arab League meeting in the early 1960s. The Arab League is where the Arab countries endorse scholarship quotas. As for the Arab World to be strategically stable shortly, they must have close connections with the African Countries as possible. These connections could only be possible through more extensive alliances on key strategic political issues and global trade partnerships.

Ramadan's last chance was to give out sensitive information the US Intelligence needed to secure his release. He began by giving elaborate details of military installations and training grounds used by the Warlords. The weapons suppliers were all available, including those who provided technical training with funding sources and persons behind the game of secrecies. Through this deal, the US team learned about the role played by Jordan and Iran in influence peddling and political interference in Sub-Saharan Africa. Satisfied with what they got, he, the guards, released Ramadan at the Kenyan Island of Pemba, where he started a new life as a mechanic to raise money and reconnect with his family. He worked ten hours each day and many times without good meals. Still, his mission was to get his family out of Somalia as quickly as possible because his arrest by US Security had significantly compromised his safety back home, exposing his identity. He had been a loyal officer to his masters, who had bestowed trust and confidence in his hands. One of his superiors, Ali Majid Issa, had links with farmers in Afghanistan who grew poppy commercially. Most of the drug is taken through Iran, Jordan, and Yemen and finds its route to the West Coast of America. Ali was famous because he owned several vessels and exported lots of honey to Jordan and Iran. He had links with many high-ranking officers in critical Government circles, and he lived a straightforward but admirable lifestyle. Ali helped many Somali youths to escape unemployment, poverty, and complex life, go live in the Arabian Peninsula, urging them to go and concentrate on their studies. He arranged for them asylum with the help of IOM through friendly countries like Canada, Norway, and Sweden, to the United States and the United Kingdom for those who were pretty read. This arrangement was in line with building a human resource that Africa will need in later years. Because we do not have fully established facilities for quality education, the best way was to relocate these youths to other better countries.

Ramadan dropped the Islamic name and acquired a new name as Phillip Githungi; his travel documents got approved by one of his clients, Musa Mohamed, a retired bus driver who worked on the Mombasa Nairobi Eldoret route for over twenty years.

Ramadan's wife Morisha was struggling back home in Mogadishu with little Shakaroni. She was running a small middle-class restaurant serving traditional and simple local Eastern African foods for the traders who ran chains of retail shops on the busy, dusty Mogadishu streets. The earnings were barely enough to buy them a decent meal and afford a modest house around town. Shakaroni was through with her intermediate level and soon joined high school, mounting pressure on her mother.

Down in Madagascar, as his friends fondly called him, Philly had adapted to life on the East African Island and knew Kiswahili, a common language. His savings were steadily increasing, and to rented an old colonial apartment and eloped some Swahili girl called Laura Maud, who worked in a confectionary shop. They cooked their meals from home, which was perfect for living within the budget. Life was moving on well, but deep in his true Somali heart, he was hatching plans of sneaking out of here and, connecting with his family, quickly relocating to another country.

This chance only seemed to get better when he serviced a Mercedes Benz for a prominent business tycoon Musa Ngeleja, a Tanzanian who hailed from the Township of Tabora; his father was once a resident diplomat in Pretoria. Musa wielded lots of influence due to the multiple trade links introduced to him by his father years ago. Those business connections helped him establish relations with his humble village of Tumbi, where they grew lots of citrus fruits and pineapples. These found easy access to Lusaka, Gaborone, and Johannesburg had connections with Southern Africa; his kids went to Cape Town and Pretoria schools. He owned some properties down south and enjoyed a lot of influence among the black business community in Johannesburg and Cape Town. He would often fly down south and stay months before returning to the small island.

One evening after a hectic day at the garage, Philly received a call from Musa asking him to travel to Pretoria, South Africa, for an assignment that later changed his life. Upon landing in South Africa, Philly received him with an Indian friend to Musa called Gohil Kumar. Kumar ran a small confectionery shop and a light restaurant for the middle class. This restaurant has many affluent customers such as bankers, medical workers, government workers, immigrants, and many young whites. Phillip was given the keys to a BMW sports and a posh apartment in the affluent high-end residential area of the rich in Pretoria's elite class.

On settling in the room and acquainting himself with a few clues by Kumar, he understood his job very well, and fitting in was not a big issue. He had access to credit cards, a fat bank account, and a few flight tickets within the region because of his long-term friend Musa. Musa was a son of a retired Country Diplomat who had properties in Pretoria, Johannesburg, and Cape Town; he was known among the wealthy, middle class and was well connected. Musa is a Russian-trained ballistics expert, while his father was an Agriculturalist turned politician.

Philly was able to get club tickets and enjoy the connections built by Musa over this period. His primary assignment was to get access to a group feared so much by the security agencies, which would later bring him to the footpath of the Caliphs. Ramadan has deliberately shopped for this job due to his earlier connections with Ali, a known undercover agent of the Caliphs. His last confessions offered him as the next best candidate for this job.

Chapter 12

ᴄᴍ

THE LINK BETWEEN THE CALIPHS
AND OFFSHORE BUSINESS

Having worked through pseudo groups and linkages with prostitutes from Johannesburg and Cape Town, Nick and Griffs bounced onto some terrible news that a criminal syndicate had hired a Malaysian ship to deliver some deadly consignment to Port Durban. But before docking with these items, the loading officials found discrepancies with the loading certificates. The original consignee was an Afro Asian called Gohil Merlin. Still, the new documents were in the names of Sky Telecoms, a company whose beneficiaries were hard-core criminals operating from the Caribbean. After checking all the information they gathered, it was now evident that Levison had placed an order for modern explosives assembled from Iran. The consignments for South Africa are for a mission codenamed "The African Chapter." Nick and Griffs combed the Ports for more details and to find out who was on the ground coordinating these moves.

On checking into a high-level Casino in Cape Town, Ursula, the Danish girl, joined their company. She is the attendant who worked at the health center where Nick got treated long ago. she was a close agent hired by Emmy. Her role was to penetrate high-profile targets before security personnel planned arrest warrants against them. She has supplied very sensitive to Linda before. She trained as a journalist, but later on, she adapted to practicing nursing, which enabled her to come face to face with many hard-core criminals. She was the one who picked the news that a strange Cargo Ship was docking sooner at Durban. Her contacts could gather clues that the documents were tampered with, and the South African Port Authorities turned it away to avoid diplomatic embarrassment. At Hilton Hotel, Nick, Griffs, and Ursula crossed to the next building that housed the Casino after parking their hired car. Inside the great Bar and Restaurant area, a posh band played strong Afro Music, and the revelers were enjoying this with no reservations. The atmosphere was so exotic with many Tourist faces around. It was a perfect place to be in at such a moment, Nick thought aloud. They moved far down the hallway and found a table for three. Settling into the comfortable seat, they waved to a waiter. Nick ordered some Fish Fillet, Italian Ice Cream, Vegetable salad, and coke, while Griffs decided on Double steak, Mexican Cheese, and a bottle of water, and Ursula opted for Rice, Fish stew, Juice, and some cake for dessert. They ate in silence and saved for a few words, only to appreciate the meal well prepared.

Nicks's mind was racing far outside the building, he wanted the finer details on his fingers now, and the issue of dinner was not customary to his style of work. Ursula had chosen this place because of the transcontinental class of clientele, but little did she say that this was a hot business hub, especially for those who wanted to pick professionals. Most mafia and security personnel dined, wined, and danced here. Nick cleared the bills as they finished dinner, and the trio walked out into the gardens for a chat. Once settled on the wooden chairs, Ursula took the responsibility of discussion leader. She informed the team that an old accomplishment sent her a personal mail alerting her about the release of the said ship by the Port Authorities, which is now heading to the Caribbean Islands of Bahama.

Maxwell Osborn was enjoying a relaxed afternoon in a hired boat with a Venezuelan girlfriend, Milka, aboard a hired Ocean liner. Two miles away was a smaller 250HP speed boat carrying four of his private security team. On the main Liner, a Mexican chef, Albert, was working his skills out preparing some Bahamian stew fish, pigeon peas, baked crab, and rice. On the deck of the ship, Osborn was sipping a strong coffee while some mutton was at arm's reach on a rolling table; Milka, on her part, was massaging his shoulders with her smooth fingers. Osborn wore colored beach shorts and a black T-shirt, while Milka donned a striped bikini and custom-made 007 sunglasses. The two were alone on the deck while a secret agent loaded with two pistols and binoculars was at the ship's tail sniffing any incoming boats; Downstairs in the crews' room were two private captains, Solo and Mick, who steered the ship well in the calm waters. Osborn was holding a Thuraya Satellite phone and a small cellphone lay on the table. The atmosphere was so perfect for ambiance. He had just communicated to T.R Roberts and informed him that cargo would land here in the Western Coasts early in the morning. He needed intelligent guys who would receive and dispatch the same in the nick of time, so the intelligence personnel prepared the necessary plans.

He had earlier talked to Smith Douglas, who ran a chain of hotels on the beaches of the Bahamas; he was an arms dealer well connected to the drug cartels in Cuba, Venezuela, and Brazil. In the U.S., he is famously called the visionary hotelier who enjoyed high-class clientele and is a well-respected gentleman for his taste for quality. He has offered services to most populists who would camp here for weeks enjoying the brisk Caribbean air; some would treat themselves to local dishes of oven-grilled fish and coconut drink.

Some young Italian couple was enjoying a honeymoon and caught a glimpse of Osborn's boat swaying deeper into the waters. On several occasions, some small ships would visit and depart after twenty minutes aboard the expensive vessel. The obscure thing was that these seemed organized moves with specific intentions. As these small boats took turns, some bags seemed loaded from the giant ship. From the strong binoculars of Marco and his fiancée Paula they could see the guys on the vessel take cautious moves on the deck with some small weapons strapped on their chests. This convolution was not a casual vessel anymore; Marco picked up his cellphone and called a friend in Washington D.C., who advised them to slowly withdraw from this area as coastline radar officials marked their coordinates on a monitoring radar. It was now a matter that needed an action with precision. Marco moved his small kayak towards a quieter part of the beach. Once ashore, stepping on the fine beach sand again with bare feet, he walked with some agitated steps pulling Paula along. They entered the small open bar and restaurant and ordered some steak and vegetables; they had a simple meal in a few minutes. Once done, they cleared their bills and dressed up in colored shirts and a pair of tour shorts; entering the sleek Landover Furiosa parked nearby, they silently drove away to an unidentified location. Deep into the hilly sides where the trees offered multiple shades, they made a stop, and Marco dialed again as he advised.

"We have picked all the info, and a team is in the air already; stay calm as we send a mission team," A woman's voice echoed on the phone. About twenty miles away, a U.S. Naval ship had finished deploying a patrol chopper with six Marine officers on board and a small military plane picking coordinates of the vessels in the target area now marked Zone A.

The head of this team is a well-trained middle-aged man in his forties, Corby. He has successfully intercepted several ships entering the Caribbean waters with contraband items like illegal weapons and gaming artifacts. His knowledge of the seas with numerous small islands harboring the fishing communities. He thought some locals here had cooperated with his team before, so getting his boys down would be easy.

Aboard the chopper, the mood was challenging because the officers had met dangerous drug dealers before, and such missions were often risky. Pulling towards the Mainland of the Bahamas, the pilot informed his team that they were about forty minutes to Zone A. The coast guards, conversant in dealing with the wrong guys, each officer began putting on jumpsuits and body cabs. Armed with each particular gun, pistol, and vision glasses, they were dropped silently at a remote and abandoned island just two kilometers away from the spy boat. Removing their own speed boat Viper 48 from the chopper, they assembled it ready for action. Corby was the first to jump onto the high-powered boat. As all officers dressed in black suits, each person with diving gears affixed on their back, they set sail immediately.

As they powered the boat towards the area, sadness wrapped the face of one of the junior officers; he was thinking ahead of the others.

Though he was combat-ready, his heart was telling him something was wrong.

Osborn's big vessel was out of vision; the waves that swept across the boat were strong enough to pull down a small powered boat. Sailing into the waters for about thirty minutes, they could catch a glimpse of the floating 250 HP boat where some private security was watching. Corby ordered his boys to switch off the engines and let the boat move on; as they were getting nearer, he pulled his diving glasses and attached the cylinders well, with a hand signal; he jumped off, followed by the three junior officers. They dismantled the boat and let it sink the body with the engine; they had already attached a small tracking device to it.

Now swimming with the maximum speed they could accomplish, Corby was the first to reach the boat; the occupants seemed unbothered as they kept drinking some rum. They were in a celebrative mood since they had overseen the offloading of cargo onto small boats about an hour ago; the team smiled as they kept smoking a white cigar with joy. Corby fixed two military-grade explosives with automatic timers onto the ship in a minute.

Osborn had known Phillip through an interface where criminals transferred a massive sum of money out of Mexico to Asia, and Phillip did this with precision using Bitcoin. He had become a reliable agent because of his connection to Rashid, who holds a Mexican passport. The two are a very deadly combination with vast knowledge of all the remote routes for merchant vessels and smaller fishing boats. They moved the numerous cays in the Bahamas that his entry into the U.S. through the Caribbean was so easy.

T.R Roberts had several business hubs that Phillip and Rashid remotely monitored. They enjoyed a cozy relationship with the girls of the beaches; they moved around as boat operators but only knew that they were a dangerous party close to hazardous operations. This group was an excellent team that was required to make grounds ready to implement the bigger plan. A considerable sum of money is needed to hire more expertise and equipment.

An order for some solar batteries and panels from Malaysia was to be shipped into South Africa ahead of the upcoming World Cup of 2010. T.R Roberts fronted a dubious Boer company for providing sound and lighting systems for all the games. Another Spanish company, known to a few called Prime, was hired to install the cameras and other security devices. The young team he recruited will help carry these gadgets to the various stadia in South Africa; it was a well-coordinated move that once these were in, another group of experts would step in and install the equipment in the restaurant's washroom, changing room, and bars. A team of electricians assembled a giant screen outside the stadium, which would attract massive soccer fans, and this was the ultimate time for Africa Project.

With rush and speed, they got a late-night flight from Gaborone to Lagos before proceeding to New York and linking up with Mike, a retired war veteran who served in the CIA before he quit the job. They are coordinating well all pointers and information gathered about the recent cargo inflows of suspected terrorists shipping arms to South America via the Caribbean through an offshore business run by a drug mogul known to be a close accomplish of T.R. Roberts. We had to travel to Kenya for a crucial meeting because Nairobi has become a hotbed for the Al Shabab terrorist attacks and with the possibility of gathering more intelligence about terrorist activities.

Chapter 13

⟲⟑⟲

THE MORAL DILEMMA OF
THE CALIPH IDEOLOGY

Keywords: Selecting the best spies, Brothels, sex and human traffickers against the Islamic laws? Iraq, Ambush, Syria, The ISIS, Counterinsurgency

الكلمات المفتاحية: اختيار أفضل الجواسيس ، بيوت الدعارة ، الجنس والمتاجرين بالبشر ضد الشريعة الإسلامية ، كمين ، سوريا ، داعش ، مكافحة التمرد ،

Alkalimat almuftahiat: aikhtiar 'afdal aljawasis, buyut aldaearat, aljins walmutajirin bialbashr dida alshryet al'iislamiat, kamin, suria, daeish, mukafahat altamarud

We had to plan another strategy for meeting the Islamic Movement ideologues who could give us some clues as to whether there is an existing Caliphate in real-time. We designed this strategic intelligence gathering at the Sheraton Hotel in Nairobi, Kenya. We chose a select group of people proficient in Arabic with the task of traveling to Kuwait, Bahrain, United Arab Emirates, Saudi Arabia, Lebanon, and

133

Iraq. However, these expeditions were high-risk tasks because they involved meeting the Sheiks and some prominent warlords. The budget for the travel could cost $60,000 for a group of five well-groomed individuals, who could carry with them three different concealed passports. The five men were: Mazuri Mamboga (AKa Ali Mahmoud), Shifta Abdallah (Somali decent), Bakari Mshoge (Aka Abdal Majid), Mokora Majuto (Aka Khalifa Abudeim) and Heri Mambo (Aka Omar Mohammad Hussein).

After our meeting at the Sheraton Hotel in Nairobi, we managed to garner support from one of the secret agents that hid his identity because he lived and behaved like a traveler. Still, peculiarly with a strikingly withdrawn character, he didn't want to mix with suspicious individuals. He had a calm demeanor and wasn't arrogant but had a laid-back personality. Moreover, he was an amiable gentleman who had a very distinctive manner of approach. He asked us whether we were traveling on a safari to the Serengeti or Naivasha national parks? In response, we said we were in transit and bound for Dubai. Excitedly, he smiled and congratulated us on our endeavors. What is your name? I asked. He smiled and simply said, Bob Joe. Have you been on a safari recently? I inquired. "No, two months ago," he answered. He dissuaded us by talking about how beautiful but expensive Dubai is. Also, he seemed knowledgeable about the Gulf States, as he just gave some conclusive hints about how to behave when you are a visitor to Dubai. For example, dealing in illegal business such as publicly walking and staggering in a drunken mood or prostitution could lead to an offense. You could call for fifty whips worth of punishment or could call for a deportation order. I believe that explains his quiet and composed demeanor.

Moreover, the following morning we went to the Kuwaiti embassy to get entry visas, and we received travelers' or tourists' visas on our passports. We then proceeded to the gulf airlines agency to buy air tickets and booked a flight to Dubai. We boarded the plane the following day. After flying for 5 hours and 23 minutes, we arrived and landed at the Kuwait International airport. We disembarked and went to the luggage room, and checked out. We boarded an airport transport bus to the Kuwait Sheraton Hotel.

The following morning we boarded a bus to Iraqi border and finally arrived at the border checkpoint. Following our reception and stamping entry visas, we embarked on the bus and headed for Basrah. On our way to Basrah, we could see roadsides littered with war machines of the Gulf wars, and we avoided some roads because they are still heavily mined with land mines, which are dangerous for humans and vehicles.

At Basrah, we encountered several black Arabs, possibly descendants of enslaved Africans. We were surprised to experience the incredible reception and warmth radiating from the population's faces. Subsequently, we were excited and proceeded to Al Basra airport and boarded a flight to Bagdad. On arrival in Bagdad, we sought to inquire how we could find Sheik Sabir Muktar. Then a kind-hearted gentleman told us to go and meet him at Falluja.

At Falluja, we met with Sheik Sabir Muktar, one of the warlords of a splinter group of the Al Qaida.

Interview (Al Hiwar al Nafsia):

What about this chaos in the Middle East and Iraq in particular?

I had to let the five gentlemen from Kenya proficient in Arabic take notes and translate from Arabic to English. Ali Mahmoud, Shifta Abdallah, Abdal Majid, Khalifa Abudeim, and Mohammad Hussein were all ready with pens and notebooks.

Sheik Sabir Muktar: First of all, I want to thank you for your interest in knowing what is happening in the Middle East and Iraq. Unfortunately, these things are happening to us all Arab nations. We are all vulnerable to terrorist attacks because we did not know geopolitics and were unprepared for chaos. However, I think those who claim to be fighting governments in Arab countries to install Islamic Caliphates act on their behalves for personal interests. The Islamic movement is interest-driven and politicized. Also, Islam is a culture and religion now but exploited by Arab nations and their allies. These allies include the US, Britain, and all European countries.

Islamic movements are bound to fail in achieving their objectives because most actors are involved or indulge in arms deals and drug cartels.

The caliph movement is an underground movement of some groups of disgruntled Muslims who have misconstrued the meaning of Islamic governance. The groups seek several attempts to install the caliph governments in regions such as Caliph Installment in Iraq, Libya (involving NATO overthrow of Gadafi), and post-Gadafi. Moreover, the Turkish politicians also want to support other offshoots of caliphs. For example, terrorists created Al-Qaida splinter group called ISIS in Syria to outmaneuver the US troops and access US weapons. In Nigeria, the Caliph is called the Boko Haram, and in Somalia, they are called Al Shabab. Thus, these are examples of the metamorphosis of the Islamic movements. They change their names and colors like chameleons. The pedagogy of the Islamic movement is that anywhere on earth, wherever Muslims migrate and settle, the caliph movement calls the country an Islamic country by default because of the presence of Islamic communities resident in their new domiciles. However, perhaps, while ignoring any multi-diversity and cosmopolitan cities in the particular country or countries of their residences, these ideologies disenfranchise and coerce the innocent Muslims living in their newfound homes.

Interview:

مقابلة (الحوار النافسة):

وماذا عن هذه الفوضى في الشرق الأوسط والعراق بالذات؟

اضطررت إلى السماح لخمسة رجال من كينيا يجيدون اللغة العربية بتدوين الملاحظات والترجمة من العربية إلى الإنجليزية. علي محمود ، وشفتا عبد الله ، وعبدالمجيد ، وخليفة أبوديم ، ومحمد حسين ، كانوا جميعًا جاهزين بالأقلام والدفاتر.

الشيخ صابر مختار: بادئ ذي بدء ، أود أن أشكرك على اهتمامك بمعرفة ما يحدث في الشرق الأوسط والعراق. للأسف ، هذه الأشياء تحدث لنا كل الدول العربية. نحن جميعًا عرضة للهجمات الإرهابية لأننا لم نكن نعرف الجغرافيا السياسية ولم نكن مستعدين للفوضى. ومع ذلك ، أعتقد أن أولئك الذين يدعون أنهم يقاتلون الحكومات في الدول العربية لتنصيب الخلافة الإسلامية يتصرفون على تصرفاتهم من أجل المصالح الشخصية. الحركة الإسلامية مدفوعة بالمصالح ومسيسة. كما أن الإسلام

ثقافة ودين الآن ولكن الدول العربية وحلفاؤها تستغلهم. يشمل هؤلاء الحلفاء الولايات المتحدة وبريطانيا وجميع الدول الأوروبية.

لا بد للحركات الإسلامية أن تفشل في تحقيق أهدافها لأن معظم الفاعلين متورطون أو ينغمسون في صفقات الأسلحة وكارتلات المخدرات.

حركة الخليفة هي حركة سرية لبعض مجموعات المسلمين الساخطين الذين أساءوا فهم معنى الحكم الإسلامي. وتسعى الجماعات إلى عدة محاولات لتثبيت حكومات الخليفة في مناطق مثل مقر الخليفة في العراق وليبيا (بما في ذلك الإطاحة بحلف شمال الأطلسي للقذافي) وما بعد القذافي. علاوة على ذلك ، يريد السياسيون الأتراك أيضًا دعم فروع أخرى من الخلفاء. على سبيل المثال ، أنشأ الإرهابيون مجموعة منشقة عن القاعدة تسمى داعش في سوريا للتغلب على القوات الأمريكية والوصول إلى الأسلحة الأمريكية. في نيجيريا ، يسمى الخليفة بوكو حرام ، وفي الصومال ، يطلق عليهم اسم الشباب. وبالتالي ، فهذه أمثلة على تحول الحركات الإسلامية. يغيرون أسماءهم وألوانهم مثل الحرباء. علم أصول التدريس للحركة الإسلامية هو أنه في أي مكان على وجه الأرض ، وحيثما يهاجر المسلمون ويستقرون ، فإن حركة الخليفة تطلق على البلاد بشكل افتراضي دولة إسلامية بسبب وجود المجتمعات الإسلامية المقيمة في موطنها الجديد. ومع ذلك ، ربما ، بينما تتجاهل أي مدن عالمية ومتعددة التنوع في بلد معين أو بلدان مساكنها ، فإن هذه الأيديولوجيات تحرم المسلمين الأبرياء الذين يعيشون في منازلهم المكتشفة حديثًا من حقوقهم وتجبرهم على ذلك.

muqabala (alhiwar alnaafisati):

wamadha ean hadhih alfawdaa fi alsharq al'awsat waleiraq bialdhaati?

audturirt 'iilaa alsamah likhamsat rijal min kinia yujidun allughat alearabiat bitadwin almulahazat waltarjamat min alearabiat 'iilaa al'iinjliziati. eali mahmud, washafata eabd allah, waeabdalmajid, wakhalifat 'abudim, wamuhamad husayn, kanuu jmyean jahizin bial'aqlam waldafatiri.

alshaykh sabir mukhtar: badi dhi bad', 'awadu 'an 'ashkurak ealaa aihtimamik bimaerifat ma yahduth fi alsharq al'awsat waleiraqi. lil'asaf, hadhih al'ashya' tuhdith lana kulu alduwal alearabiati. nahn jmyean eurdatan lilhajamat al'iirhabiat li'anana lam nakun naerif aljughrafia alsiyasiat walam nakun mustaeidiyn lilfawdaa. wamae dhalik, 'aetaqid 'ana 'uwlayik aladhin yadaeun 'anahum yuqatilun alhukumat fi alduwal alearabiat litansib alkhilafat al'iislamiat yatasarafun ealaa tasarufatihim min 'ajl almasalih alshakhsiati.

alharakat al'iislamiat madfueat bialmasalih wamusaysata. kama
'ana al'iislam thaqafat wadin alan walakin alduwal alearabiat
wahulafawuha tastaghiluhum. yashmal hawula' alhulafa' alwilayat
almutahidat wabiritania wajamie alduwal al'uwrubiyati.

la buda lilharakat al'iislamiat 'an tafshal fi tahqiq 'ahdafiha li'ana
muezam alfaeilin mutawaritun 'aw yanghamisun fi safaqat al'aslihat
wakartilat almukhadirati.

harakat alkhalifat hi harakat siriyat libaed majmueat almuslimin
alsaakhitin aladhin 'asa'ua fahum maenaa alhukm al'iislamii.
wataseaa aljamaeat 'iilaa eidat muhawalat litathbit hukumat
alkhalifat fi manatiq mithl maqari alkhalifat fi aleiraq walibia
(bima fi dhalik al'iitahat bihilf shamal al'atlasii lilqadhaafi) wama
baed alqadhaafi. eilawatan ealaa dhalik, yurid alsiyasiuwn al'atrak
aydan daem furue 'ukhraa min alkhulafa'i. ealaa sabil almithal,
'ansha al'iirhabiuwn majmueat munshaqatan ean alqaeidat tusamaa
daeish fi suria liltaghalub ealaa alquaat al'amrikiat walwusul
'iilaa al'aslihat al'amrikiati. fi nayjiria, yusamaa alkhalifat buku
haram, wafi alsuwmal, yutlaq ealayhim aism alshababi. wabialtaali,
fahadhih 'amthilat ealaa tahawul alharakat al'iislamiati. yughayirun
'asma'ahum wa'alwanahum mithl alharba'i. eilm 'usul altadris
lilharakat al'iislamiat hu 'anah fi 'ayi makan ealaa wajh al'ard,
wahaythuma yuhajir almuslimun wayastaqiruwn, fa'iina harakat
alkhalifat tutliq ealaa albilad bishakl aiftiradii dawlat 'iislamiat bisabab
wujud almujtamaeat al'iislamiat almuqimat fi mawtiniha aljadida.
wamae dhalik, rubama, baynama tatajahal 'ayu mudun ealamiat
wamutaeadidat altanawue fi balad mueayan 'aw buldan masakiniha,
fa'iina hadhih al'ayduyulujiaat tahrim almuslimin al'abria' aladhin
yaeishun fi manazilihim almuktashafat hdythan min huquqihim
watujbiruhum ealaa dhalika.

What is Iraq's demographic divide?

The Iraqi demographic divide lies in three categories, but these
three divisions are not the cause of the crisis in this endowed country.
These three groups include Shia Arabs, the majority branch of Islam,
living in the south of Iraq. However, in the North and West are the
Sunni Arabs who compose the Sunni Muslims. The capital Bagdad is

a mix of Sunni and Shia. Moreover, in the far north is the Kurds, that are Sunni by a majority, but ethnicity divides them from Sunni Arabs. The Iraqi government is predominantly Shia, and the disgruntled Sunni Arabs minority that comprises ISIS extremist group controls much of the country. In addition, the marginalized Kurds that suffered oppression during Saddam Hussein's regime took advantage of the upsurge of ISIS and demanded regional autonomy.

Interview about the Caliphate and Battle of Karbala, 680 AD

Sunnis and Shias have gotten along fine for most of Islam's history, but the Syrian and Iraqi crises are driving them apart today, and it helps to understand the historical roots of how Islam split along these two major branches and what it has to do with Iraq. In the 7th century, soon after the Prophet Mohammed, who founded Islam, died, there was a dispute over who should succeed him in ruling the vast Caliphate he'd established. Some wanted to elect a successor, while some argued power should go by dividing birthright to Mohammed's son-in-law, Ali. The dispute became a civil war, the divide of which began with today's Shia (the Partisans of Ali, or Shi'atu Ali, hence Shia) and Sunni. Ali was killed in the city of Kufa, in present-day Iraq. Twenty years later, his followers traveled with Ali's son Hussein from Islam's center in Mecca up to Karbala, present-day Iraq, where enemies killed them in battle, and the war ended. Their pilgrimage was mapped here; it made Kufa and Karbala, and other locations in southern Iraq, the heartland of Shia Islam.

However, modern Islam has taken another route of War Lords. A warlord is a leader able to exercise military, economic, and political control over a subnational territory within a sovereign state due to their ability to mobilize loyal armed forces. Usually considered militias, these armed forces are devoted to the warlord rather than the state regime. Warlords have existed throughout history, albeit in various capacities within the political, economic, and social structure of states of ungoverned territories.

مقابلة حول الخلافة ومعركة كربلاء ، 680 م

اعتنق السنة والشيعة معظم تاريخ الإسلام ، لكن أزمتا سوريا والعراق تفرق بينهما اليوم ، وهي تساعد على فهم الجذور التاريخية لكيفية انقسام الإسلام على طول هذين الفرعين الرئيسيين وما يتعلق به بالعراق . في القرن السابع ، بعد وقت قصير من وفاة النبي محمد الذي أسس الإسلام ، كان هناك خلاف حول من يجب أن يخلفه في حكم الخلافة الشاسعة التي أسسها. أراد البعض انتخاب خلف له ، في حين أن البعض جادل بأن السلطة يجب أن تذهب عن طريق تقسيم حقوق المولد إلى صهر محمد ، علي. أصبح الخلاف حربًا أهلية ، بدأ الانقسام بين الشيعة اليوم (أنصار علي ، أو شيعو علي ، ومن هنا الشيعة) والسني.

Muqabalat hawl alkhilafat wamaerakat karbala', 680 m
aietanaq alsanat walshiyet mezm tarikh al'islam, lkn 'azmata suria waleiraq tafaraq baynahuma alyawm, wahi tusaeid ealaa fahumi aljudhur alttarikhiat likayfiat ainqisam al'islam ealaa tul hdhyn alfareayn alrayiysiayn wama yataealaq bih bialeiraq. fi alqarn alssabie, baed waqt qasir min wafat alnabii muhamad aldhy 'usus al'islam, kan hunak khilaf hawl min yjb 'an yukhlifuh fi hukm alkhilafat alshshasieat alty 'assha. 'arad albaed aintikhab khalf lah, fi hyn 'ana albaed jadil bi'ana alsultat yjb 'an tadhhab ean tariq taqsim huquq almawlid 'iilaa sahr muhamad, eali. 'asbah alkhilaf hrbana 'ahliatan, bada alainqisam bayn alshiyet alyawm (ansar eali, 'aw shieu eali, wamin huna alshiyet) walsiniy.

قتل علي في مدينة الكوفة ، في العراق الحالي. بعد مرور 20 عامًا ، سافر أتباعه مع حسين علي بن الحسين من مركز الإسلام في مكة إلى كربلاء ، التي تقع في العراق حاليًا ، حيث قُتلوا في المعركة وانتهت الحرب. يتم تعيين حجهم هنا ؛ جعلت الكوفة وكربلاء ، وغيرها من المواقع في جنوب العراق ، معقل الإسلام الشيعي.

Qutil eali fi madinat alkufat, fi aleiraq alhali. baed murur 20 eamana, safar 'atbaeuh mae husayn eali bin alhusayn min markaz al'islam fi makat 'iilaa karbala', alty taqae fi aleiraq halyana, hayth qutlu fi almaerakat waintahat alharb. ytmu taeyin hajihim huna ; jaealat alkawfat wakarbala', waghiruha min almawaqie fi janub aleiraq, maeqil al'islam alshiyei.

وه بـرحـلا ءارمأل .بـرحـلا ءارمأل رخآ آقـيرط ثـيدحلا مالسإلا ذختا ، كلذ عمو ةيسايسلاو ةيداصتقالاو ةيركسعلا عساـعلا ةرطيسلا ةراـسم رداق ىلع ميعز ةئـبعت ىلع مهـتردق بـبسب ةدايس تاذ ةلود لخاد نطونـي نود نم ميلقإ ىلع ىلإ ربتعت ام ةداع يتلا ، ةحلسملا تاوقلا هذه .ةيلاوملا ةحلسملا تاوقلا

بالحرب أمراء كان كانت. الدولة لنظام تسيير ولبرحاء لأمراء المؤاتية ، موليشيايات
موجودون على مدار التاريخ ، وإن كان ذلك في مجموعة متنوعة من القدرات
المختلفة داخل الهيكل السياسي والاقتصادي والاجتماعي للدول أو
المناطق غير الخاضعة للحكم.

Wamae dhalk, atakhadh al'islam alhadith tryqana akhar li'umra'
alharb. 'umra' alharb hu zaeim qadir ealaa mumarasat alsaytarat
aleaskariat walaiqtisadiat walsiyasiat ealaa 'iiqlim dun wataniin
dakhil dawlat dhat siadat bsbb qudratihim ealaa taebiat alquwwat
almusalahat almualiati. hadhih alquwwat almusalahat, alty eadat
ma tuetabar milishiat, mualiatan li'amra' alharb walaysat linizam
aldawlata. kan 'umra' alharb mawjudun ealaa madar alttarikh, wa'iin
kan dhlk fi majmueat mutanawieat min alqudrat almukhtalifat dakhil
alhaykal alsiyasii walaiqtisadii walaijtimaeii lilduwal 'aw almanatiq
ghyr alkhadieat lilhukm.

Thank you, Moulana (honorable) Sheik, for your brief and concise
introduction of the root causes of turmoil in the Islamic faith. We
prepared to head for Baghdad but were warned by our host to be
careful because bandits infested the roads. Thank you, sir, Griffs
responded. The following morning we set off for Bagdad in convoys
of twenty vehicles with armed security forces, which we gave some
baksheesh (bonuses) for their food, cigarettes, and other amenities.

The Ambush

In about Forty-five kilometers, the first convoy came under attack,
and we saw plumes of thick black smock rising in the middle of the
road. Our driver shouted at us to get off the vehicle and run for cover.
While scampering for cover, the car behind us came under fire, and we
could hear: Allah wa Kubarr! Allah Wa Kubarr! La'ee La'ee la la la…
The assailants seemed to take what they wanted and dashed
away into the dried-up former gullies that had swamps. The valleys
provided good cover for the bandits. Our driver kept conversing with
the security forces, but I did not understand the conversation. Then
our translator asked him to explain what was taking place despite the
bombs and gunfire had not seized to rattle. "Walahi, kulum haramiat.

Mafish mana, ashan iftekir au aetakhidu, huum fil Hala jeid wa lakin, idha shurta dharab, haikun mashakil, imkin haiktuluna kula…" those were bandits, we don't have to worry much, but I think their conditions are good. If we responded, I think they could have killed us all." Respond by our driver. However, if our security forces returned fired back, it could have been very bad. Why? Griffs asked. There are many holed-in those gullies, and they could have over-whelmed our forces. They could kill all in this convoy. Who are these bandits? Griffs inquired. "Most of them are warlords comprising former Sadam Husein's soldiers and other offshoots of Al-Qaida. They do things like that for a living," said the driver. The journey commenced again, but this time, three armored Humvees that were supplied for every convoy led the convoy. We were scared but assured that security was at its maximum now because authorities provided three more armored vehicles to take us back to Bagdad at the front of the convoy.

At Bagdad and expedition to Karbala

We arrived at Bagdad fresh and assured of safety by the convoy commander. We decided to book a hotel room at the Sheraton for two nights. The nights were tranquil, and the breeze was gentle overnights. We had to plan for another trip to Karbala, but we also wanted to know how many people were traveling in a convoy bound for Karbala. It was a harrowing experience from our last journey that shook us when our convoy was shot at by bandits who dashed away into the galley terrains. On the third day, we embarked on the new journey to Karbala, one of the longest convoys. We traveled for two hours, and at a specific marshy location, the convoy came to a stop. The panic of terrorist attacks again revisited us.

Moreover, this was one of the worst ambushes we have ever experienced. The terrorists seem to be experienced combatants who cut the convoy in three segments. We were all boxed in. while the front vehicles came under fire with several vehicles hit with RPGs and in plumes of black smoke, we were surprised when the second vehicle in front of our car got hit. The noise of the bomb was deafening, and all of us jumped out of the cars to take cover. The same happened from the convoys behind and last vehicles. All we could hear were rattling machine guns, as though there were enormous fireplace crackling and occasional sounds of Poom! Bloom! from the Rocket Propelled Grenades (RPGs). The convoy was pinned down for two hours when we finally got rescued by the military units from both sides of the cities of Bagdad and Karbala. There was a lot of damage done to the convoy on this unfortunate expedition. We recovered with lots of panicky moods and ringing eardrums. We inquired how far Karbala could be from where we were because we wanted to return to Bagdad in fear of what could be lying ahead of us. Then one knowledgeable security personnel who was one of the escorts spoke to us encouragingly:

"Do not lose hope because we expected these things, which were the reasons why the convoy is heavily escorted today by many security personnel. The bandits probably expected things to be easy today because many travelers get robbed on this highway often. Today they also took many casualties because we could decimate their strongholds from where heavy mortar shells came from by carpet shelling or artillery bombardment. It's a big lesson for them; they will not forget this day. We declare this day a victory, Inshallah." The convoy made its final journey to Karbala under heavy escort with three Armored Personnel Carriers (APCs); one at the front, another in the middle, and the other at the rear.

Karbala's excitements and horrors

The convoy arrived in Karbala at around 3 pm, and we had to lodge at an affordable, secure hotel for at least two days. We had a good supper and slept well. In the morning of the following day, after eating breakfast, we asked one of the hotel guides to take us to one of the most revered mosques to meet a cleric. The guide hesitated first and expressed uneasiness that it could be dangerous because most of the clerics connived with some warlords. Furthermore, since we were a mix of Westerners and Africans, there could be a high suspicion because terrorists perceive your presence as an espionage act. However, we assured our guide that we had no connections with any governments, but we are Islamic scholars researching the Caliphate Empire that was said to have existed in Babylon. Our guide nodded but with lots of skepticism. We offered to pay him USD 100, and he accepted but warned us of any eventualities. So we started and toured several mosques that included; the Holy Shrine of Imam, Hussania, the holy mosque of Karbala, and Imam Ali Mosque. We were warmly welcomed at Imam Ali's Mosque and had a few words with the cleric. However, we did not want to sit for more than five minutes, and the imam saw us off. On our arrival, one guide took us on a tour of one of the famous mosques, the mosque of Kufa. It was one of the ancient Shia mosques known for many centuries. It was built in the 7th century, home to Ali Ibn Abi Talib and the Rushidun Caliph.

The mosque has historic remains of the Maytham al-Tammar, an area of interest to our most extraordinary expedition. We were warmly welcomed at Kufa mosque by a good number of clerics who were interested in our mixed-race group. One of them asked us whether we intended to convert to Shia. According to him, "Shia is the only true world religion, and we wish every race in the whole world will one day convert all into this holy faith. Then there will be peace in the whole world". We smiled at him, patted him on the shoulders, and told him we were interested in this holy shrine because it has one of the world's old religious buildings. After listening to our account of the need to document good things from such historical sites, he was excited. We then decided to leave after spending about twenty minutes at the site. The clerics warned us that we should be careful because there are criminals who are unhappy about other religions and could target foreigners.

The suicide bomber and many deaths

We left the shrine and headed downtown. The suspicious-looking police stopped our driver and ordered us to get out of the vehicle. There seemed to be some coordinated responses, and to our surprise, we were surrounded by many civilians comprising women, children, and older men. The driver signaled to us that it could be our tours to mosques that may have alerted and excited the city. As police were interrogating us at a checkpoint, some men dressed in clerical attire looked at us with queer looks. However, we paid no attention to them, as the police were beginning to understand the motives of our visits.

We were shocked by one young boy in his teens that came into the crowd, but the locals recognized him as a terrorist operative.

Some of the groups began running away, but it was too late when the teen pulled something from around his belt and shouted, "Allah Wakubarr!" then a bomb went off. We fell at the thunderous Poom! Boom! sound. The aftermath of the bombing was very horrendous. So many injured civilians were groaning, and some were crying because of sustained injuries. Many dead bodies and casualties lay on the ground. The police were perplexed at this juncture, but they were brave to calm the terrified victims and survivors of the suicide bombing. Then we were released by the police and asked to go away as soon as possible to avoid another suicide bombing. However, the police first examined us for any kinds of injuries from the shrapnel of the bombing. We only sustained bruises and were nursed for the wounds. We left without asking many questions, but we later asked our guide and driver why we came under such a suicide bombing attack? Our guide explained: "The general security situation in this country is very fluid…people live by faith. There are many warlords after the fall of Saddam Hussein, and the truth about religious hatred has become overt. I suspected the suicide bomber was an assassin from within the localities and one of those trained to fight religious intifada against fellow Iraqis or foreigners. When they saw you, they suspected you of being Americans, and you know that they hate Americans here". We thanked our guide and apologized for putting his life in danger. We offered him another $200 as a token of appreciation. We finally reached the hotel where we spent the last night.

We asked our guide specific questions about whether there are Brothels, sex, and human trafficking part of the terrorist networks or if these are against Islamic laws? Why do several religious extremist groups exist in unstable countries like Syria, where ISIS is active? How about the motives of counterinsurgency in combating such lawlessness? Well, I think you have asked me heavily loaded questions; firstly, though there are no brothels in Arab countries, which I cannot speak for all, what we know secretly are that there are brothels in some European countries where some of the wealthy Arabs go to for sex tourism. In answer to the second question, ISIS is one of those splinter groups of Al-Qaida groups founded on countering foreign invasions, but their operations are pretty fussy because most of them are mercenaries per se. They fight for foreign powers that have helped overthrow some governments or fight proxy wars. For example, Al-Qaida was the best ally the Americans used against the Soviets while the Russians had their troops in Afghanistan. Thus, the claim that Caliphate Empire installations are the agenda of ISIS or Dahesh is all hypocritical and fallacious. On the question of counterinsurgency in combating lawlessness in troubled countries, it's pretty enigmatic to presume that counterinsurgency is a way out, but one thing I must make clear is that the Western countries have hands in creating instabilities in those troubled countries. When an arms race destabilizes a developing country, the military-industrial complexes in the West profit from the sales of arms to the country at war. In addition, wars cannot be dubbed with Islamic Caliphates or in some parts of the world, especially the developing countries; wars are tribal wars because politicians use tribalism as part of their political hegemonies. Therefore, those who claim they are fighting to install Islamic Caliphates are lying about their economic interests that underscore the plights of the countries in anarchy. Those are all that I can tell you from what I know. Thank you, sir, for enlightening us about everything you have to explain. We then prepared to travel to our last destination in the following expedition; this time, we were going to Lebanon.

Beirut-Lebanon

Following our last expedition in Karbala, we flew to Bagdad by chartered plane and booked a flight to Lebanon. In about one hour, we boarded a plane to Lebanon, and after three hours, we landed at Beirut airport. When we arrived in Beirut, the aiport service men guided us to the Sunni-dominated part of the city, and we secured hotel rooms in the vicinity. Beirut city is three specific religious locations; east for Christians, West for Sunni Muslims, and south for Shia Muslims. The majority of city dwellers of Beirut exhibit façade in their daily living activities unless provoked by unusual events. Some of the extraordinary events are conjured by fanatic sectarian groups of people who unleash terror with lightning owe. Omar, one of our entourage, visited one of the neighborhoods in the Shia-dominated suburbs. Here is Omar's story of survival:

"One afternoon, I went to the suburbs of southern Beirut for shopping. Upon arrival, I asked where I could buy brass kettles and trays. One kind-hearted stranger directed me to one of the stores, and I went to check for prices of some goods. At the time, I did not have enough money to purchase the items. They were quite expensive because they were labor-intensive. As I left the store, I met one of the familiar gentlemen from the other suburbs. He immediately shouted in excitement, Omar! Keifak (in Arabic greetings: how are you?). However, before I could answer him for a few minutes chatting, an older man was stooping with a sizable stick. The older man stood bent and in a stooping position. He asked me, what's your name? I answered Omar. The older man shouted in a peculiar voice to alarm residents. AhWawawa…Ulululululu…Thief! Thief! Within a few seconds, I saw the street filled with angry youth with various weapons. Some carried machetes, others swords, yet others clubs. I raced away, and when they spotted my direction. Boy! I never ran like that in my entire life. It was a race for survival, a matter of life and death. The mob chased me until the bridge marked the border between Lebanon and Syria. The bridge was my rescue frontier; otherwise, they could have hacked me to death." It was blatant and violent mobs who were in a hot pursuit that could have resulted in hacking into pieces my whole body in an exercise of unquenchable hatred. Holy cow!

That was a sectarian hatred; I didn't know how the Shia hated the Sunni to that magnitude of toxicity. When I met an indigenous Sunni man from the Lebanon side of the bridge and narrated my ordeals to him, he said: "you needed to consult with the locals first to decide to cross to the other infested part of the city. They could have celebrated the murder of an infidel and promoted those who participated in the violence. You know Omar is a Sunni name and could easily put your life in danger when you go to Shia-controlled neighborhood."

Sectarianism is counter Caliphates.

The most crucial test of all times in the history of Islam is the two divisive sects of Sunni and Shia denominations. When we inquired about the reasons behind those divisions and their general implications on the Islamic faith? The clerics were a bit iffy in explaining the basics, but one exciting philosopher in the Islamic faith who asked for anonymity of his interviews explained in a very succinct manner the reasons for those rifts; prophet Mohammad for Sunni and Hussein for Shia. He alluded to all those sectarian movements as politically motivated. For example, Hezbollah (Party of God) is a political wing that is linked to the Palestinian cause. "How could God have a party?" He asked such a question simply because using Allah's name weighs in by rallying many militants. It's a brainwashing concept. Allah is Allah. Allah is not a weak Allah, but not to be politicized, Walahi, and those who indulge in such abominable acts will face judgment inshallah.

Following our last and exhaustive expedition, we bid farewell to the clerics who wished us well throughout our endeavors to find the truth, but they cautioned us not to indulge in religious politics because nothing is clean about it.

Turkey Caliphate revisited

Following our guide's advice, we set off on another exciting expedition to Turkey. He appreciated our offers in terms of money and felt he could help us in any possible way. We had to plan ahead of time by contacting the Turkish embassy in Bagdad and familiarizing ourselves with the tourism industry in Turkey, including historical sites. Also, the conceptual banality of disguising ourselves as tourists was a cover-up that could disarm secretive attention from the diplomatic receptionist. Omar Mohammad broke the impasse by playing and laughing excitedly to add more decoys. "Isn't this much different from the safari in Kenya?" he asked. Well, it's certainly different because we will visit the world's historic places.

The receptionist asked how many days we would want the tourist visas for one month or two? We responded by saying we wished to get visas for a month. The receptionist jokingly retorted, 'you guys seem to be good tourists; why can't you go for a three months visa?" In awe, we looked at each other's eyes, and as though we knew the correct answer, we all nodded in unison. "Three months visas accepted," Omar answered. We handed in our passports and paid the visa fee alongside.

Our visas were approved in about fifteen minutes, and we received our passports from the receptionist. The receptionist was beaming with infectious smiles, and she softly said, "I wish you a safe and happy tour of Turkey, a great country". We responded in a chorus, Thank you, madam. We left the embassy and boarded a taxi to the airlines' agency to buy and book a flight to Ankara, Turkey. Following our booking, it was already 3 pm. We had to go to the hotel and relax and avoid the sweltering heat. So, we were as brittle as gecko lizards because 48°C was just as good as a frying pan.

When we arrived at the hotel, we cooled down with some refreshments of orange juice. We relaxed and watched TV on the Dr. Phil's show that was running an interesting canceling program of an old American lady the Nigerian 419 scammer scammed. The evening went smoothly, and we ordered our dinner, roast lamb with fresh arugula salads mixed with other fresh greens. After spending the night the following morning, we called a taxi that drove us to Bagdad airport to board the Turkish Airlines. After three hours and a half of airborne, we landed at Ankara airport.

In Turkey, we went to the famous Kocatepe mosque in Ankara, the capital city, and we met a brave cleric who spoke to us in a modest elocutionary manner. The cleric's gesture can identify his status with the confided expression of a high-profile and charismatic Islamic scholar. We felt lucky to bump into such a living library.

We briefly introduced ourselves and how many countries we have traveled to in seeking the history of the Islamic Caliph. In response, the cleric who did not want to reveal his real name asked to be called Shakh Hajj Moulana (honored titles). We asked him whether an Islamic Caliph existed in modern Turkey.

Thank you, the faithful, for taking painful decisions and resources in your quest for holy but pilgrim journeys to sacred lands or cities where Islam once thrived. I'm privileged and opportune to give you some answers to the best of my knowledge about what Islam was once upon a time, a formidable and holy crusade or jihad.

However, I must first begin by saying this: Islamic fundamentalism is becoming insidious in aspects of disrupting peace around the globe. That's to say, it's proceeding gradually, subtly, but with harmful effects. These groups of Islamic ideologues at certain times were known as the

Khalifat movement, an Indian Muslim movement that lasted from 1919 to 1924. This group evolved in response to counter the sanctions against the Caliph of the Ottoman Empire after the First World War by the treaty of Sevres between France and the Ottoman Empire. The Kalifat movement was a political protest campaign intended to restore the Caliph of the Ottoman Empire, a Sunni Muslim.

Moreover, in these modern times, Islamic fundamentalism has become as polluted as the global warming phenomena. There are many racketeers, gullible followers, and worst of all, those who have turned Islam into business endeavors. It's a big shame when naïve and gullible youngsters go around Europe and bomb or kill the innocent in the name of Islam; it brings shame to the whole Islamic faith. The truth of the matter is the cliché of brutality set out by the minority of the lost youth that does not address the fundamental issues causing the moral decadence in the faith. It's, therefore, the moral responsibility of the few honest clerics to revitalize modern Islam that is not swayed by politics or business ideologies.

In addition, the fundamental ideology of the Caliphate was the restoration of the empires that Islamic kings ruled, but it got weaponized by criminals to terrorize the world. That's the point of departure of the neo-Caliphates movements, which have mushroomed almost everywhere.

You have mentioned the revitalization of Islam as not being bent towards politics or commercial ideologies; what did you precisely mean by those strong but sensitive expressions?

"Well, I may be misquoted by some Islamic scholars, but let's call a spade a spade rather than a spade a spoon. When we consider those two analogies, a spade scoops much more on earth than a spoon. Thus, the truth can liberate us all when we tell the truth". Correct! We chorused.

"You see, the world has become too corrupt and difficult to live in because of bad politicking through oppressive governments whose repressive regimes nudge the commoners into acting criminally. I mean, in oppressive governments where economies become volatile, and there are public dissatisfactions, what do you expect? There is going to be high crime, turmoil, and violence. That will be followed by poverty and corruption. I would perhaps want to say that those clerics who turn Islam into political and commercial platforms are mere survivors of enduring hardships. Therefore, the theory for restoration of the Islamic Caliph is a façade for recruiting terrorists that have to respond by fighting fraught and repressive regimes without attaining Islamic values, but they have added insults to the injuries upon the already high-jacked Islamic faith. Thus, Islamic terrorism is funded by warlords and racketeers to destabilize corrupt and repressive governments".

Thank you for your precise and concise presentation of the historical facts, which may be challenging to research. Mr, Griffins encouraged the Sheikh for his brief time and for being honest. We would want to know your opinion on the issues of political Islam that led to the split of India and Pakistan or Bangladesh. Whether or not it's feasible in the current geopolitics?

"Well, that will be another topic when you come back next time, inshallah." The Sheikh replied.

"Thank you for your time again; inshallah, we will return shortly, and may Allah give you peace." Mr. Griff responded. Then we bid farewell with hugs and cheek kisses and set off to the Ankara airport.

Chapter 14

⌒⁓

THE WORLD CUP 2010 SOUTH AFRICA

The Blueberries and Oregano

As early as 2006, strange shipment activities were taking place along the South African Coasts of Durban and Port Elizabeth; the unfolding vents seemed more rapid than ever. Airports, Hotels, and beaches were busier with an extensive network of flights from big international carriers and small charter planes. Many tourists took the opportunity to fly down South as hotels and banks cashed in on the increased trade volume. Flights were getting overbooked, but no one seemed to care about what was happening; as long as they were making money, they could afford to be lazy anyway.

Several new migrant laborers were filling up the streets of Johannesburg, Pretoria, and Durban; what was pulling them into South Africa was a new wave sweeping across Africa after the Country was declared the host of World Cup 2010. Events were moving very fast that didn't make meaning to ordinary people since they would not reap much from the much-hyped games.

Down in Cape Town, a meeting is taking place and facilitated by T.R Roberts with his team. The forum is progressing in a private residence in the affluent suburbs or the West Coast. All instructions were issued for many big Hotels to be scanned by his special agents to see possible areas for carrying out a dirty mission; many people were unaware of the secretive event. They discussed in great detail the stadia and marked their seating capacity, exit routes, special facilities like bars and restaurants, changing rooms, and medical facilities. These were marked Blueberry trees, the place for multiple explosives. The major tourist hotels and beaches were marked as Oregano, where the squad would implement nerve gas attacks, and this is where they would deploy the hired girls.

Women and young girls were being recruited and trained as bartenders and escort girls; none knew their specific roles as their instructors did not disclose them at this time. So many young girls who are job seekers went from South Sudan, Somalia, and as far as the Philippines were promised jobs at various hotels, beaches, and nightclubs across South Africa. Several young boys were specially selected and trained by Phillip as drivers and stewards.

T.R. Roberts ordered solar batteries and panels from Malaysia through his numerous offshore agents. The orders were then consigned through an Iranian vessel registered in the name of a Taiwanese Mogul Fe Ming into South Africa in containers of pharmaceuticals disguised as medical supplies.

The secretly consigned solar battery shells were with loads of highly explosive material. The whole battery cages were sealed with 5kg each of explosives with automatic timers linked to circuit breakers already installed within the solar system.

T.R Roberts has always had a bitter heart for The US Government for capturing several of his offshore businesses and freezing considerable sums of money he had amassed through several of his numerous dubious business empires. Roberts lost many of his most trusted friends looking for an opportunity to teach the World a lesson, and such a chance does not come easy. He hired crooks from a dubious Boer company to provide sound and lighting systems for all the games.

He used his influence in the underworld business network and secured a Spanish company only known to a few Prime to install the cameras and other security devices. He met Luigi while in Barcelona and how they executed a brilliant cocaine deal was so soul-touching that he could not leave behind such a precious contact.

At a particular time, Luigi blew up a warehouse in Milan when a drug deal went wrong, and the Italian Police caved in on them. To escape arrest, he set off the hidden bombs they had in their planned escape car, killing several people, and he became a wanted person in Italy with a 5m USD bounty for information leading to his arrest. Because of his vast knowledge of the secret service and Police, he slipped away just like an eel. Many people fear him because of his astute composer, sharp vision, and action. He later settled in Zimbabwe and lived a simple life as a fake farmer as he lay below the Interpol radar. He married a Ndebele woman with whom they sired two kids and lived west of Harare.

Luigi now took personal supervision and screening of the young team recruited to carry these gadgets to the various stadia in South Africa. It was a well-coordinated move that once these were in, another group of experts would step in and install the equipment in the restaurants, washrooms, changing rooms, and bars. A team of technicians will assemble a Giant screen outside the Stadium, which would attract a massive number of soccer fans. The moment was the ultimate time for Africa Project codenamed Blueberry!

The equipment arrived on cargo and lighter freight ships under companies disguising their consignments as educational materials, medical supplies, and rice. The main aim was to avoid the security teams on the ground, T.R Roberts had secured all fixtures of the matches and venue. They had known which games would be played in which Stadium and the estimated number of fans.

All information is analyzed by Luigi and the execution team to assess areas with maximum impact. He had suggested to the Mission Boss that they preferred to carry out a sarin gas attack which they identified could be procured through Jordan and moved into the mainland through their pharmaceutical group. The squad argued that the gas attack could leave several dead, and the attackers wouldn't need to be within the premises of the explosives. In addition, the explosives could place many of their hired agents at risk of being near the scene of the attack, yet T.R. Roberts preferred the use of assembled explosive devices.

Various companies started getting into the Stadia and were working 24/7 to ensure that the World Cup was a success, the first of its kind in South Africa as host, a bid which had taken many years of lobbying and campaign. The explosives almost went off as some thought either Algeria or Tunisia could take this chance. As South Africa won the bid to host this world cup, several activities changed strategies from banking, airline companies, tour companies, and Global intelligence systems as many countries sent secret servicemen and women down South.

Nick was ahead since he had a better knowledge of the geopolitical structures in South Africa, so he positioned his agents with great caution. He was aware T.R. Roberts was no dead donkey to play around with, so he selected one of his best-seasoned personnel to monitor events here. Roberts had deployed in Cape Town, Johannesburg, and Port Elizabeth. He left Pretoria to an old friend who knew the game of underworld operations very well.

At the Soccer City in Johannesburg assembled on the 11th of July 2010, when Spain played knock out with the Netherlands, a big crowd had gathered at the Stadium as early as 10:00 am. In the hotels and restaurants, several undercover prostitutes mingled easily with soccer fans and tourists.

A group of young tourists was enjoying the morning swimming in the lavish pool, and they were oblivious of what was happening in the World as they enjoyed canned beers at the poolside bar. Some were in the rooms enjoying cozy moments with the young black girls. Sonia, one of the girls, had been hooked by a tall British pensioner Freddie. They were on the eleventh floor, cuddling and kissing, romping, and with lots of alcoholic drinks on the table, they cared less about the outside World; as they slowly chewed each other's lips, a blaring shooting scene came up on the 40-inch screen. Immediately the confusion brought them to reality; Freddie jumped out of bed and dialed the British Embassy in South Africa, seeking clarification on what was happening. The British Embassy informed him that a terrorist group had penetrated the Country and was seeking to cause havoc on foreign nationals, especially Americans and their close allies. Freddie dismissed Sonia with a hundred-dollar bill as he rose to dress. He called Emmy, alerting him of an extensive scheme of nasty guys on the ground. Emmy relayed this information directly to Linda, who was hosting a group of business partners at a fake party at a hired venue.

Nick received a message via his satellite phone from Linda that an anomalous activity was occurring at the Eastern Port, and he immediately rang Griffs. Linda has been living here for over five years, disguising herself as a Health worker helping many rapes and drug abuse victims. She managed to get endorsed on a Lions Club membership, a position she used very well to meet many influential people in the security circles and business network. Nick had provided her with a list of possible targets, and she picked the information needed with the accurate precision of a hawk. Nick then alerted a close confidant in The White Hawk of South Africa about a suspicious cargo offloaded at Port Elizabeth whose freight documents were highly protected from the clearing agents leading to a brawl. As officials fought for supremacy and authority over who should be allowed onto the ship, sooner a shootout began. Agents on board the vessel were armed with automatic weapons of higher firepower and alerted to get ready for action.

In a short time, they had overpowered the Port Authority Security, and they pulled powerful Audis from the ship and drove off in a mighty convoy of six cars with guys who were all heavily armed, leaving 32 dead in their trail. They drove in powerful Audis and Range Rovers in different directions, giving the Police a harrowing chase.

Police helicopters provided aerial coverage in tracking these rascals, and communication was being relayed to the several police units across the Country about a nasty group being busted with cruel intentions to cause a massive murder. Television Stations were covering the events live, giving details of a terror attack with vast loads of explosives captured at Port Elizabeth, sending the World a great shock. US marines who had camped in a leisure resort along the Western Coast of Cape Town swung into action by installing their remote satellite and communications gadgets to begin eavesdropping on communications from the White Hawk and South African Police.

No one had anticipated an outrageous atrocity of this magnitude. The events that happened on 9/11 in the US sent a new global terror alert to the CIA, MOSSAD, and Secret Service in the UK. Tel Aviv sent 4 F-15 jets into the sky destined for South Africa, while US Naval War Ship Alexander 2 sent over 5 B-2 bombers into space to watch over the troubled Country.

Over 25 police and military helicopters have been activated and sent into the airspace. Military jeeps and armored vehicles ferried Ground troops with several secret service members in private cars sprawling towards the East Coast, Pretoria, and Johannesburg. But the team with a different mission was headed by Nick, and they drove to Cape Town, where T.R. Roberts and Luigi were meeting top agents for their mission.

T.R. Roberts held a black leather bag full of money in 100 US dollar bills, which he handed over to Luigi, saying: "This is 5 million cash, and I have a card here with another 5 million on it, and the pin included in the envelope, all I want is a total success." As he made this statement, a helicopter flew in their direction, and they heard police cars with sirens from a distance.

As members in the room scampered for the exit doors, Nick and Griffs were already on the compound wearing body armor. Both men were armed with automatic rifles; a shootout started as police cars pulled in, giving more fire support. In the ensuing confusion, Nick managed to detonate a smoke grenade, and he blew off the southern door and hurled it into the living room. There were no occupants here, but gunshots continued coming from the hallway down, leading to the several bedrooms ahead.

This impasse lasted three hours before more police and military personnel came over to give backup. The White Hawk arrived atop military jeeps with more sophisticated weapons for the counter-terrorism unit. Inside the house were more than two dozen agents under T.R. Roberts command deputized by Luigi. The squad of the recruits was holed in here, and they were the ones giving the Police tactical headache with greater firepower. Luigi wanted to blow up the house with all the occupants, but his automatic switch remained in the Audi car parked outside. No one had expected this immediate lead by the Police since many of their activities and bookings were conducted through proxies or undercover agents.

Harold from the police ballistics squad went on all fours to smash a door further on the left, and he sprayed several bullets before two men shouted," Hold on the fire," as they came out with hands over their heads. Griffs joined in quickly, handcuffed the captives, and took them to the police cars outside. Actions of shootouts preceded the serenity that resulted in fatalities. Luigi was found dead in the lavatory, and he lay over with a black leather bag on his bullet-riddled chest; Nick took the bag and handed it to Griffs.

The search continued, and over six dead bodies were recovered and found in pools of blood along the corridor, and more than a dozen who were wounded were then handed over to the Police.

Several hours before, a contact in Pretoria had sent a buzz message to T.R. Roberts about the shooting at Port Elizabeth and the ensuing scuffle between his agents and security personnel. Roberts received information about how his guys killed the Port Authority security and the vengeance with which Police and paramilitary responded. However, his men emerged victorious and were trailed by the security team all over.

Upon hearing the police sirens and the sound of a helicopter draw nearer, T.R Roberts left Luigi and about a dozen survivors in the living room and entered a room with a hidden maintenance hole linking to an underground tunnel; he vanished before Police and Nick reached him.

Why must criminal syndicates and mercenaries become victims of their actions? One police man asked while nodding his head. I wish we captured them all alive so that interrogations could be thoroughly conducted. Now we might miss some good information for the forensic department to analyze and piece together all the dots. He wondered.

Printed in the United States
by Baker & Taylor Publisher Services